QUEEN TAKES CAMELOT

JOELY SUE BURKHART

For my Beloved Sis

Thank you to my comma warriors and beta readers:
Sherri Meyer, Kaila Duff, Lydia Simone,
Bibiane Lybæk, Jennifer Swan, Beth DiLoreto, Ashleymarie Petke,
and Amanda Pierce

QUEEN TAKES CAMELOT

A THEIR VAMPIRE QUEEN NOVELLA

This expanded version includes
Queen Takes Avalon!

The Once and Future King has always been my curse.

You think King Arthur is a hero.
You blame me for the fall of Camelot.
Because I refused to choose.

Yes, I loved Lancelot. Once upon a time, I loved Arthur, too. I loved all of his friends, even Merlin, the cantankerous wizard.

But Arthur's jealousy destroyed our love. He smashed the Round Table, banished Lancelot, and locked me in a burning tower. He would rather see me dead than love another man. Even his best friend.

So now I'm doomed to repeat this grim tale over and over until Arthur wins my love. But this vampire queen will never choose Arthur. Not after what he's done. I will certainly never choose him over Lancelot.

I will never settle for just one knight. Not when I can have them all.

Oh, and this time? Arthur will be the Once and *Dead* King, because Camelot is mine.

1

LANCE

I felt so fucking *useless*.

Four. Hundred. Years. Of waiting. Aching. Needing. Straining to feel my queen anywhere in the world.

I knew she was out there. Somewhere. I could feel her existence in the soft whisper of wind, the sparkle of starlight, and the melody of the rain.

Guinevere lived. My queen needed me. And I was unable to go to her.

I didn't know why she hadn't called me to her side, though I could guess all too easily. Most likely, she wasn't *free* to call me. Or she was protecting me.

I refused to consider that she might have given up on me after so many lifetimes of failure.

I had failed her and she'd died, not once, but many times over the lifetimes of our curse. My beautiful, generous, laughing queen's life snuffed out by bitter jealousy.

We were doomed to live out the same tragedy each life-time. I'd lost not just my queen, but also my best friend and many of our other companions. The Round Table had never recovered. Camelot had fallen. Lancelot of the Lake was no more. On the bright side, neither was King Arthur. The man who'd killed our beloved.

The man I'd tear apart with my bare hands on sight.

In this lifetime, I had never been her knight, let alone her champion. The once famous Sir Lancelot had been reduced to hiding in a goddess-forsaken hellhole in the middle of nowhere and attempting to drink myself blind.

Urgency ground my bones to dust. Tension constantly strained inside me. Desperation warred with helplessness. I needed to go to her. I had to do something. Even if I had absolutely no idea where she was, or worse, where our enemies were, I was certain they waited for the slightest hint of a misstep.

Scowling, I tapped my empty glass on the bar. The bartender shot me a wary look to judge how drunk I was, shrugged, and poured me another shot. A human might have been poisoned by so much alcohol, but it didn't affect most of my kind beyond slowing us down. A couple of drinks dulled the ragged edges of my nerves, a fucking blessing even for a few hours. But I would have to be careful. I never knew when the call would come, and the last thing I wanted to do was show up incapacitated to a fight.

And there would be a fight. There always was. We always died. Selfishly, I preferred to die first, because I fucking hated watching my queen die. But it was inevitable, until we figured out how to break the cycle.

Even with the roaring desperation lowered to an urgent hum, I still wanted to pound some steel, crack some skulls, and drain the blood from a couple of humans.

Risky thoughts that would damn my soul before I could ever find Guinevere. We Aima had few rules that we had to live by but feeding on humans was an unforgivable sin. The goddesses had given us great power and magic, but we couldn't feed on humans, or risk eternal damnation.

Queens provided the stability, structure, and yes, the blood upon which we fed. Without my queen...

I was a walking, talking time bomb. It was nothing less than a fucking miracle that I'd made it this long.

I heard the door thump open behind me, but I didn't turn around. Heavy steps approached in a cadence that I knew well, even though no chainmail or spurs jingled. Not here in this modern world of cars and cellphones.

The man leaned against the bar and jerked his head at the bartender, who immediately dropped a cold beer in front of him.

In the original legend, Bors was supposedly my cousin. In this lifetime, we weren't related by blood or house at all. Yet somehow Bors and I had found each other, even without our queen's call.

There was an echo between us, a resonant memory of all that had passed before. He was one of the good guys. I could trust him. Even with my queen. I knew it, as surely as I knew that Guinevere lived again. She had loved him once upon a time. She would love him again. As I did.

For nearly four hundred years, we'd roamed the remotest places that remained on earth, trying to stay sane and free, until our queen could call us.

"You're late," I said gruffly, turning to face him.

About my height but thicker with solid muscle, Bors was dressed like a modern human in ripped, worn jeans, a plain white T-shirt, and heavy motorcycle boots. He wore his dark hair buzzed short, giving him a mean, fierce look. Not that he needed any help looking tough with all those tats covering his arms and the scar across his forehead.

Without answering, he tipped his head back and drained the bottle in one long swig, opening his throat so the liquid poured into his body without the need for swallowing.

He fed exactly the same way, preferring to puncture the

biggest vein and guzzle the resulting fountain as it poured down his throat.

My cock throbbed. It'd been entirely too long since either of us had fed, but we had to be careful. Most Aima could sniff each other out over time, especially if they were feeding. At heart, we were predators. Blood on the air was just as attractive to us as chum in the water for sharks, and Aima blood carried a special pheromone that was a dead giveaway to our kind.

I couldn't remember all of the other lifetimes I'd lived out this dire curse, but betrayal was always at the core of my failure to save Guinevere. It wasn't that I distrusted Bors, not at all. But if we were together, it would make it easier to kill two of our queen's Blood before she could even call us. Until she sealed our bonds, we had no power. While we were physically stronger and faster than humans, we couldn't shift until our queen's blood flowed in us.

Which made us nothing more than pawns on the Triune chessboard, easily picked off and leaving our queen exposed.

However, pawns had the freedom to move on the board at will, and so that's what we did. We stayed away from each other to maximize our coverage on the playing field, while staying out of any other queen's reach. Because that was definitely something I'd learned long ago.

Some queens called a Blood for love. Others called a Blood for power, regardless of the Blood's desire to serve her. A queen could force a bond on even the most unwilling Blood if she was determined enough.

The memory of being trapped in such a Blood bond lifetimes ago still made knives twist deep in my stomach. I turned back to the bartender, grabbed what remained of the bottle, and headed for a table in the corner.

Another man sat with his back to the wall, watching the room without moving a muscle. Even though we hadn't come into our power yet without our queen, Mordred could hide in plain sight. A trick of light and shadow, or simple illusion, I wasn't sure. He wasn't invisible—but he could make my eyes skip right over him if I wasn't paying attention.

He'd been fucked over by history too. If Guinevere's adultery was blamed for Camelot's fall, Mordred was labeled a traitor and Arthur's death laid at his feet. Most stories had him killing the great king and dying on the battlefield. Sometimes he was even Arthur's son. Some said he'd tried to steal the throne from Arthur, while he was away trying to kill me for falling in love with Guinevere. Others had Mordred marrying Guinevere, which was closer to the truth than anything else.

I took a seat opposite him, and Bors sat between us, positioned to keep an eye on the door. Mordred had chosen a remote island off the coast of South America as his hiding place. Bors roamed Tibet. I'd chosen the Gibson Desert of Australia, our current meeting place. I was sure more of the original knights were in the world somewhere, but in most of our lifetimes, I hadn't encountered them. They weren't as close to her as I had been, or even Bors or Mordred. I had to assume they'd already died in the long years of this lifetime.

These men were my brothers. Bors, my lover, when we were together.

We hadn't seen each other in a decade, yet I still didn't know what to say.

The only people other than our queen that I cared about were Merlin, Arthur himself, and Elaine Shalott. Arthur would kill me if he had the chance, especially if he could find me before Guinevere was able to call me to her side.

Elaine...

Cold sweat broke out on my forehead. My sanity

wouldn't survive another encounter with her. Not in this lifetime. I'd rather be dead than serve her again.

But my queen...

I couldn't abandon her to her fate again. I had to stay free. Which meant I had to gather as many of her Blood as I could.

I knew where Merlin was. Which meant either Arthur or Elaine would be nearby, waiting to spring the trap. Maybe both of them. They'd joined forces before.

"Any news?" I finally asked Mordred. He might be on a remote island in the middle of nowhere, but he always knew court dealings. I had no idea who his contacts were, and I didn't know if he'd tell me even if I asked.

"There's a new American queen. Triune's running scared."

Bors grunted beneath his breath. "I'm not buying it. The Triune doesn't fear anything."

Mordred lifted a ceramic coffee cup to his mouth and took several sips. How the man could stand to drink hot coffee in the middle of the desert, I had no idea. "They fear Isis's last daughter."

Bors whistled softly. "Well yeah, shit. I would guess so. Where'd she pop up from?"

"If they know, no one's saying. My guess is they *can't* say."

I pushed the whisky bottle away from me. If we had to wade through Triune shit to find our queen, then I would need all my wits about me. "Who's strong enough to lay that kind of geas?"

"The queen's mother, I'm guessing. Evidently the daughter's existence is a bit of a shock. She's strong too. My contacts say she's already been to Mexico and was headed to New York City to deal with House Skye. North America will be hers, and with a solid foothold in Mexico, the rest of the Americas may soon follow."

"Could she be our queen, then?" Bors asked. "Guinevere was always fearless like that."

I exhaled and allowed my eyelids to flutter shut. Blocking out the world, I strained with all my will to reach my queen. To pinpoint her location. Anywhere. A hint of where she might be. What she was doing. If she was well...

I strained until my heartbeat thudded heavily in my skull.

Shaking my head, I sat back heavily in my chair and opened my eyes. "If she was our queen, surely I'd be able to feel her. Especially if she's as strong as you say."

"Since she's already taken several Blood, I don't believe this queen is ours." Mordred set his cup down before him, though he wrapped both hands around the ceramic as if warming himself. "I choose to believe it's a sign. A sudden new queen. Shifting power struggles. Someone even the Triune fears. The tide is turning. I have to believe that means our queen will be free. Soon."

"We must be ready," Bors said, his voice shaking with emotion.

Yeah, me too. My heartbeat raced. Even though my mind cautioned me not to get excited. Not to hope too much. We'd been devastated so many times before...

But this felt right. Hope burned in my chest. This time, it would be different. I'd find her. I'd save her from Arthur. We'd break the curse. Somehow. I refused to consider anything less.

"The real question is do we risk trying to free Merlin now?" Mordred asked softly. "Or do we wait and hope she can call us first?"

My hope crackled with ice, shards that cut my heart to ribbons. I didn't answer right away. I wasn't necessarily the best one to make this decision.

Alphas weren't supposed to be afraid, or to hesitate to make a decision that affected his queen and the rest of the Blood. But alphas weren't meant to be forced into service and raped, either.

Elaine Shalott had taken me by force—not in this lifetime, but in many previous ones. My blood, my bond, my mind, and yes, my body. Numerous times over the centuries. The thought of falling back into her control made every muscle in my body rebel.

The risk was astronomical for all of us. If our queen's alpha was taken by another, what hope would Guinevere have of defeating Arthur and breaking the curse? How could the rest of her Blood defend her if they had no alpha to guide them? But if I went to our queen's side with only three Blood…

She might not be strong enough to protect us all. In all likelihood, we'd be defeated yet again. She'd had ten Blood before and we'd failed.

Because we hadn't been complete. We hadn't freed Merlin.

The legendary wizard had been locked in Avalon since before Arthur had even cursed us. Over the many lifetimes since, we'd failed over and over. Guinevere died. We died.

Merlin was the key. We needed him. Our queen needed him.

But if we failed to free him…

We'd die before she could even call us, and a queen with no Blood of her own would surely die too.

"I say hell no," Bors said, his voice as hard as steel. "We know he's crucial, yes. We'll all die without him. But we've tried to free him before and died. We can't risk dying before she calls us. Or worse, if we lose Lance to *her*, then how can our queen possibly defeat her?"

"We have to face the probability that Arthur already has our queen," Mordred whispered. "Perhaps that's why she hasn't called us."

Rage surged through me, a hot, thick flood of hatred and fury that choked me. As much as I dreaded the thought of ending up in Elaine's control again, I'd rather serve her indefinitely than lose Guinevere to Arthur again.

"No," Bors retorted. "I refuse to even consider it."

"We—" Whatever I'd meant to say died on my tongue. My head rang like I was standing in the top of Notre Dame while Quasimodo clanged the bells all around me.

The call.

My queen.

My senses locked on her halfway around the world. I couldn't hear her voice in my head, not until I tasted her blood, but she tugged on me like the moon drags the tides.

I was on my feet racing for the door. Someone grabbed my arm and I whirled, ready to tear the offending hand from his body for daring to slow me down.

Bors. I lowered my fists, though I still vibrated with the call. Finally. *Goddess above, thank you.*

"We go together," Bors said, squeezing my arm until I nodded. The chances of one of us failing to reach her would lessen if we protected each other's backs. It made perfect sense, even while I screamed internally because they weren't moving quickly enough.

Mordred threw some bills down on the table to cover our drinks and slipped past me through the door. "What the fuck is taking you so long?"

2

GWEN

E ngulfed in flames, I screamed his name until I had no voice left.

Lance!

Lancelot du Lac.

My lover. My alpha. My Blood.

But he never came. He couldn't. None of them could.

I knew it was a dream, but I still couldn't wake up. My eyes burned from the smoke. My skin charred, split, and tore away. My lungs throbbed with pain. The building slowly crumbled around me...

Wake up!

Panting, I jerked upright in bed.

I swallowed down the useless tears and frantic cries. The pleas for help. They'd done me no good then, and they certainly wouldn't help me now.

I flipped on the bedside lamp, even though exhaustion ground through my body. I rarely slept because of the nightmare.

I remembered being burned alive—by my husband. Or rather, by *her* husband, my cursed ancestor, Guinevere.

The man of legend, lauded for his honor, had murdered me. Everyone knew the story of King Arthur, the once and future king. They remembered Camelot, his knights of the Round Table, and how Queen Guinevere had destroyed it all with her adultery.

Unfortunately, everyone preferred to forget the earlier accounts of his story that had been quietly brushed away over the centuries. Like how he'd fathered a child on his sister, and then to hide his misdeeds, he'd murdered dozens of boys born on the same day as Mordred.

Or how he'd locked Guinevere in a tower and burned her alive.

People preferred to forget the atrocities a powerful man could do to a woman when he wasn't well pleased with her.

I would never forget, and goddess help me, this time, I would have justice.

The memory of Guinevere's death was engraved in my soul, even though it hadn't happened to me. I was descended from the original Guinevere and cursed to relive her suffering until her tragic ending could be righted. Somewhere out in the world this very moment, the man who'd been King Arthur walked and breathed, looking for his lost queen, driven by his jealous rage to find me and claim me as his. I could only count myself lucky that in the last three hundred and seventy-three years, he hadn't found me.

Or maybe he had found me years ago but had decided to wait until he could punish my lover too. Because Lancelot du Lac lived again. My destiny, the cruel love triangle I'd been relegated to live by history. Only there weren't three sides to this love story. Guinevere had loved Arthur once upon a time, and she'd certainly loved Lancelot. But she'd also loved Merlin, and several of her king's other knights as well.

She'd refused to give up Lancelot, or any of her knights, which was why Arthur had burned her in the tower. If he thought I would choose him over my knights, wherever they were…

I would kill him myself as soon as I laid eyes on the bastard.

My cellphone rang, jarring me so much I almost knocked it off the nightstand trying to grab it. I didn't recognize the number. "Hello?"

"Gwen, are you alright?"

I recognized her voice, and now that I knew it was Shara Isador, my new queen, I felt her bond shimmering with concern inside me too. She was far to the west, headed back to her home in Eureka Springs, Arkansas. In a matter of days, she'd killed the former queen of New York City and then flown to Egypt to kill the sun god, Ra.

Leaving me in charge of the biggest city in America as her queen sibling, with hundreds of former Skye sibs to sort. That wasn't a complaint. I was actually thrilled with the prospect of such an organizational challenge. "I'm fine. Are you home already?"

"Soon." Her bond swelled inside me, and I braced for her to take control of me. She was the stronger queen. There was nothing I could do to hold her at bay if she truly wanted to push her way inside me. She'd know everything, see everything, feel everything.

I wasn't trying to hide anything, and I was truly grateful for everything she'd already done for me. She was a saint compared to both of my former queens. Keisha Skye had tortured her alphas and made her entire court watch, and Elaine Shalott…

Just thinking of her made me quiver with rage.

Shara's bond quieted inside me and she withdrew her power without forcing her way into my thoughts. "I felt your pain, and I was worried."

Her compassion—not just for the pain she'd sensed, but

for not forcing her way into my head—made my eyes fill with tears. "It's only an old nightmare."

"Only?" She asked doubtfully. "The pain was horrible. Not just the physical pain, but…" Her breath sighed out. "The betrayal."

Oh yes. I knew betrayal all too well.

"How close is Lance?"

Relieved that she changed the subject, I concentrated on my approaching Blood. They burned like white-hot fires inside my mind, blazing light and love and urgency as they raced to me. I knew one of them was Lance, and that he had two others with him, but I couldn't be sure who they were. Not yet.

If only I could feel Arthur the same way. If I could warn them *before* he attacked. Or if I could be on the lookout myself. But I felt and saw nothing else amiss, even with the additional power Shara had given me with her blood.

Until I had my own Blood… My powers would be limited.

"Close," I whispered hoarsely. "Hours away yet, but they're approaching quickly. I think they'll be here by noon tomorrow. Or rather, today."

"You mentioned earlier that what I'd heard of the legends wasn't the truth. Are you in danger, Gwen?"

I clenched my jaws a moment, fighting down the urge to wail and scream at the same time. I was afraid, yes. I was scared shitless. But I was also beyond furious. My rage burned inside me like a tangible flame I could feel scorching my bones. "Yes, always. The curse repeats itself every generation. I'm torn from my Blood by Arthur because he can't bear for me to love another. Even if Lance reaches me, I'm afraid we still might not survive. You probably should have listened to Carys and chosen another sibling to hold your city, Your Majesty."

"Shara," she said firmly. "And no. I chose exactly who we need in New York. Have you ever had a queen sibling before to help you fend off Arthur?"

"I don't know. I can sense the past like a winding, endless river flowing through me, but I can't see all the bends and twists. I know the curse is his doing. I remember dying at his hands over and over and over. I remember losing Lance. I remember Arthur cutting off each knight's head while forcing me to watch. Once, Elaine Shalott had Lance collared like a dog and there was nothing I could do to free him. She was stronger than me, because Arthur had refused to allow me to take my Blood."

"But how could he do that? You're a queen. He shouldn't have any power over you."

"Do you know what an Aima king is?"

"Ah. That makes sense then. He can shift at will without a queen, so he's unpredictable and even more dangerous."

"Exactly," I replied grimly. "His beast is always a red dragon. Merlin saw him fighting a white dragon before Arthur's birth, and the red dragon always wins."

"And you're the white dragon."

"Supposedly, though no queen in my house has survived long enough to claim her power in several generations."

"Well, this time you have Isis's daughter at your side, as well as Coatlicue's daughter. Plus hundreds of siblings that we've claimed for House Isador. You have a foundation of power to draw from whether your Blood arrive or not. So use it. Use us."

I blinked, unable to comprehend what she was offering. A strong queen didn't offer her power to her sibling. Not like this.

"I mean it, Gwen." Her bond inside me shimmered with opal moonlight, but it wasn't soft or gentle. It cut like a glass. "This isn't your battle alone. You have sisters ready and willing to help you. If you think my dragon can help fend off Arthur, then we'll turn around and fly right back to New York City in the morning."

I didn't know what to say. I'd never had someone actually offer to help me. Not like this. "My queen."

"Shara," she repeated firmly, though I could hear the smile in her voice. "You're not alone, Gwen. Not this time."

I swallowed the sob down, but tears still streamed down my cheeks. "Thank you. You don't know what this means to me."

"I do," she said softly. "I was alone for most of my life. I'll be home in another hour, two at most. The trip is taking us a bit longer than we planned. Should I be present when your Blood arrive? I can have Gina ready the jet and we'll fly back to you as soon as we reach Eureka Springs."

I didn't answer right away. My knee-jerk response was to insist that she stay put. I wasn't used to asking for assistance. But this was bigger than me or my pride. If I could save Lance and the rest of my Blood by accepting my queen sibling's assistance, then I'd go down on my knees and kiss her feet if that's what she wanted.

But Shara had just faced danger I couldn't even begin to comprehend. She'd need time to heal and recuperate, and a much needed few days of rest in her nest would probably do her a world of good. "I'd hate for you to come all the way back here so quickly. Lance is close. If I could reach out to you…"

"Of course, my bond is always open to you. At the first sign of trouble, draw on my power. We'll light the fuckers up."

I let out a started laugh. "Sounds good. I owe Arthur a very large bonfire."

"Then it's a very good thing you've got a queen sibling whose gift is fire." She laughed, but her voice echoed with the dark, furious power of a goddess's retribution. "No one's going to hurt one of mine and get away with it."

"What about Elaine?" My voice cracked on her name. "I still carry her blood."

Centuries ago, House Camelot and House Shalott had come to an agreement that was supposed to end the bad blood between our families. Our once powerful houses had both withered over the years thanks to the endless curse that killed our queens. Children were harder and harder to sire, especially queens, and I'm sure my aunt feared that if I died, House Camelot would disappear for good. She'd delivered two sons, but never a daughter. Mama had lived for decades with that generation's Arthur, and I'd come to believe that she'd relished escaping that life with her death. I never knew if she'd had a chance to love her Sir Lancelot or not.

I'd only been thirteen years old when I was given to Elaine to be her pet. For that was exactly what had happened, despite my aunt's good intentions. Elaine had gained me and both my cousins for her Blood. She'd sworn to never kill me, and in exchange, my aunt made me exchange blood with Elaine.

She couldn't have known that Elaine had been dabbling in dark magic.

I still remember standing there before her, barely more than a child myself, and watching the smug look of hatred on her face as she made me swear on my own blood that I would never call Blood of my own.

Denying me Lancelot. The man she'd coveted since the legend's beginning verse.

Shara had broken that oath with her blood and her power, but I still carried Elaine's blood, and she carried mine. I could feel exactly where she was, and without looking at a map, I would be able to fly and then walk straight to her.

I didn't need GPS to know that she was near Glastonbury

Tor. She knew its importance all too well. Eventually, I would be forced to walk into her back yard.

Because the gate to Avalon—and my dear Merlin's prison —was through the Chalice Well.

"What I take, I keep, remember?" Shara laughed lightly, but her bond weighed heavily inside me, winding through me like the white dragon of my supposed gift. "I've taken you as my sibling. If she doesn't that, she can deal with me. And if she thinks about interfering with my sib's Blood..."

I held my breath, and it felt like the world stilled, waiting for her answer.

"Then she will learn what it's like to anger a queen who deals in death and darkness."

3

GWEN

Like Shara, I despised the ostentatious ballroom the former queen of New York City had used to conduct her business. I hated gold-leaf anything, and massive chambers of cold marble and soaring ceilings hand-painted to look like the Sistine Chapel had one use only.

Intimidation.

Thank the goddess, House Isador didn't care to use such tactics. Shara had used a very comfortable study for her sibling interviews, and so would I. Though I had one problem to address.

The last place I wanted to be when my Blood arrived was on the one hundredth floor.

Until I shared blood with Lance, or at least physically touched him as he came through the protective barrier, he wouldn't be able to cross into Shara's blood circle. Since her phone call, I'd paced and stewed for hours, running scenarios through my head. My vivid imagination all too easily saw Lance and whoever else he'd brought with him standing on the sidewalk outside, smiling with joy...

Only to be cut down from behind by Arthur.

He had to be here. Somewhere. He wouldn't rest until Lance was dead. He'd lie in wait like a poisonous spider, waiting to strike. I couldn't leave my approaching Blood standing outside unprotected for very long.

Finally, I decided to hold court in the lobby downstairs. It'd been open to the public in House Skye's days, but Shara had eliminated all non-Aima people inside the tower. So there really wasn't any reason I couldn't sit out in the open area and meet the last few potential siblings. The chairs were actually rather comfortable, and since the building wasn't open to the public any longer, the lobby was as quiet as the study upstairs. Plus, I could stare out the plate-glass windows and watch for my Blood's arrival.

My stomach knotted with anticipation. Hunger. Desire. Terror. All tangled up and simmering with tension. Lance was an hour away. Maybe less. I could almost feel the ground trembling beneath his feet as he rushed toward me. But the closer he got, the tighter the noose around our necks. The only sure place Arthur could find my knight—would be at my side.

The young interim consiliarius, Kevin Bloom, cleared his throat to politely draw my attention from the windows. I liked his cheerful personality and his attention to detail, but Shara and her primary consiliarius weren't sure how far we could trust him yet. They'd left an assistant with us to help out, though I was sure she was primarily to keep an eye on Kevin and report any difficulties or issues to our queen if she had any doubts of his trustworthiness.

"Who's next?" I asked, keeping my voice even despite the nerves tumbling inside me.

"Gawain Gwyar of House Igerna."

I froze, fighting to keep my face smooth and calm. Gawain. Could it be?

I watched the man approaching me and I couldn't deny

the surge in my power. Something inside me recognized him. But how could one of my Blood have been so close to me this entire time and I'd never noticed?

He was dressed in a modern gray suit. The jacket molded to his broad shoulders perfectly. He towered a foot over Kevin, certainly built like a knight of old, though his face was hard, as if he'd been chiseled from granite.

Kevin gestured at the chair opposite me. As Gawain started to sit, he hesitated, turning his head to look at me. His eyes flared. I watched as his face transformed from wary politeness to shock to a sudden blast of joy. Brilliant blue eyes locked on my face and he stiffened, jerking around to face me.

"My queen? Is it really you?"

The pulse of magic was undeniable. I definitely recognized him. But…

It didn't feel right. I couldn't explain it. Gawain had been one of Lance's closest friends and certainly one of Arthur's best knights. Guinevere had loved him dearly. After Lance, there were several Blood that I would be ecstatic to call, including Gawain, though my alpha was the crucial piece to our curse.

He took a step toward me, but I lifted my hand. He immediately stopped, which I took as a mark in his favor. "Sit, please. I have some questions for you."

He did as I asked, though he sat on the very edge of the chair, his body tense. He leaned toward me as much as possible. His shoulders quivered, and he gripped the arms of the chair fiercely, as if fighting to keep himself in position. "Ask me anything, my queen."

"How long have you been in the tower?"

"Since the first of the year. My house sent me as tribute to Skye."

Only a few weeks, then, but still, the thought of one of my Blood being so close, and I'd never felt or sensed him…

Even if it'd been Elaine's geas, surely I would have felt him as soon as Shara's bond took over. Yet he'd been nearby for several days and I hadn't felt him in the slightest.

"I had no idea," he whispered, his eyes stricken with guilt. "Forgive me, my queen. I would have come to you immediately. Why couldn't I feel you?"

I made myself relax back against the chair and smile, even though wariness coiled in my stomach, ready to strike. "A geas was put on me centuries ago. I wasn't allowed to call any Blood until recently."

"The Isador queen broke the geas?"

Keeping up the illusion of ease, I reached out toward Lance, trying to guess how close he was. Minutes away, I was sure. But he was outside the circle and this man was inside. If this was Arthur…

My blood chilled in my veins. Lance would arrive to my call, only to watch as Arthur claimed me. Or killed me.

I smiled wider, trying not to let my eyes flash with fury or determination. There was nothing in his manner or appearance that signaled he wasn't who he said. I couldn't quiz him about the real Gawain, since there were elements about Guinevere's life that I didn't know either. It wasn't a perfect rebirth every single time. Events changed us.

His eagerness slowly dulled, and his shoulders slumped. "You don't recognize me. Do you feel me at all? Am I so changed over the years?"

I studied his face, searching for anything I could recognize and know beyond a shadow of a doubt. He was handsome, apparently earnest and honest. Young, I thought. Aima could be difficult to age, but he felt no older than Shara's alpha. Not even a century. Surely Arthur would feel… heavy with power and intent.

"A man can change, my queen," he whispered. "Time has no master."

And I knew then, without a shadow of a doubt, that he couldn't be Gawain. There had never been any reason for Gawain to say such a thing. Renowned for his courtesy and defense of women in the early accounts, his character had only picked up inconsistencies in later legends. Gawain wouldn't have felt the need to make any kind of excuse for himself. He hadn't needed to change. There was nothing for which I would have needed to forgive him.

I didn't move to defend myself, but he must have read the realization on my face. Sighing softly, he gave me a sad smile. "You always were too smart for your own good."

"Only a man who's intimidated by a smart woman would say such a thing."

"Touché." He leaned back in his chair, giving up the earnest eagerness act. Instead, he sprawled in the simple chair like it was a grand throne. He widened his knees, taking up more space, but also putting his package on display. Not that I was interested. "You can't fault me for trying. I knew that if I came to you right away or openly that you'd doubt me. I hoped I could show you the truth before you leaped to our unpleasant past."

Kevin looked at me, his brow furrowed with concern. The suddenly innocent sibling interview had gone off the rails, and he had no idea why or what we were dealing with. I didn't know if I could trust him to help, though I didn't know what a mostly-human consiliarius could do against a king of Arthur's renown. Kevin wasn't even a formal Isador sibling, so he wouldn't be able to bring Lance through the circle.

I met Arthur's gaze and said coolly, "That's a strange way of admitting that you murdered me."

Paling, Kevin flinched and his eyes widened. He fumbled

for his phone and backed away, but I didn't know what he could do. Even if he called 911, the police wouldn't be able to enter. Besides, what could they do against a dragon king?

:Shara, I need help.:

Without hesitation, she pumped me with power, so much that I couldn't help but shiver. Goddess. I didn't envy her in the slightest. Carrying that much power was exhausting, and the cost... It took a personal toll, whether she realized it or not. Through our bond, she looked at the man sitting across from me.

:He's already inside the circle. How do I get him out, and let Lance in at the same time?:

Her bond shimmered like a pearly sword inside me. *:We fucking push him out.:*

4

GWEN

I needed to bleed. All this power flowed inside me thanks to my queen, but it wouldn't do any good until I found a way to release my blood. Magic always required a sacrifice, and for Aima queens, that meant our blood, blessed by the goddesses themselves.

My fangs were too obvious. At the first flash of white, he'd be on me before I could even taste a drop of blood on my tongue. I wore a necklace of a crescent moon with one end sharpened to a point for exactly this purpose, but Arthur knew that trick all too well. As soon as my hand fluttered up toward my throat, he'd pounce. I didn't want to give him an excuse to attack before Lance and my Blood arrived.

Concentrating fiercely, I tried to warn them, even though they didn't carry my bond yet. *Beware. The king is here.*

"You, human." Arthur waved his hand carelessly over his shoulder. "Go stand by our queen where I can see you."

Clutching his notebook fiercely, Kevin walked back toward my chair and took up position on my right.

"Put the phone away."

I glanced up at him and tried to smile soothingly. "Do as he says, please."

"Of course, Your Majesty." His voice trembled, but Kevin slipped the phone into his pocket. "I take it this gentleman isn't Gawain Gwyar of House Igerna after all?"

Arthur gave us his most charming smile. "Technically, I am Gawain. Or rather, he's in me. Since I ate him."

I closed my eyes a moment, fighting down the wail of rage and loss. One Blood dead before I could even see him with my own eyes.

"It's the honorable ones who are easy to find." Arthur continued as if he was describing what he'd eaten for break-fast at a five-star restaurant. "Gawain never thought to change his name, or at least leave his house's nest and spare them my wrath. I'm sad to say that House Igerna has gone the way of House Skye in that regard."

"Only our new queen didn't kill and eat everyone inside House Skye." My voice quivered slightly, but I refused to show him how much his words hurt. "Who else have you murdered?"

"The un-honorable ones have been harder to find," he continued without answering my question. "But I knew they would eventually come to you. Traitors always do. I'm not pleased that Elaine's geas held them off so long, but no matter. That gave me plenty of time to find the rest."

"What do you want?" I knew, but I hoped to keep him talking. My mind raced, trying to come up with a plan. If I waited until my Blood arrived... Nothing changed. Not without blood. If I made the slightest move, he'd be on me. His casual posing was all a sham.

"It was so considerate of you to agree to meet with me here." Arthur tipped his head at the glass walls. "Perhaps we can come to an agreement with Lancelot before things get... nasty."

People walked by outside, rushing to their jobs and appointments like it was any other day, too busy to peek inside the building that they couldn't enter.

But all too soon, beloved faces would appear at the windows, unable to step inside.

Lance would never come to any agreement with Arthur. Not after what had happened. Neither would I, for that matter. But if I played along, maybe something would come to me. "What kind of agreement?"

Arthur leaned forward, radiating sincerity. He braced his elbows on his knees and loosely clasped his hands. He wore a large gold and onyx ring on his wedding finger.

My throat closed off, my brain flinching away as the past reared its ugly head. I remembered when Guinevere had slipped that heavy ring on his hand. She'd loved him in the beginning, though she'd come to despise him before the end.

His ring had fueled his ego. The ring he'd given her in exchange had been a prison. A life sentence in hell. And that had been before he realized she was in love with his knights too.

"Be my Guinevere, like we were always meant to be."

I swallowed the cold, hard knot trying to choke me. "You know that has never worked."

"It will this time," he insisted. "I've changed, Gwen. I really have. I understand what I need to do to please you this time."

Even when he tried to be sincere, he was still an ass. He made it sound like *I* was the one at fault for centuries of torment. Me.

The one he'd burned to death in the tower.

I was being difficult. You know, insisting that he not run around killing our friends and their entire families. Silly me.

"If you want him, you can have him."

Eyes narrowed, I searched his face. A muscle ticked in his cheek and he gripped his hands together firmly enough that his fingertips were whitening. "You can't even say his name, so why on earth would I believe that you'd allow me to have him?"

"I made a mistake in trying to keep you from him. I know that now. I still don't like it, but if it means I can have you, then I will share you."

It was a huge concession for a man like him, but I still didn't believe him. His voice had roughened, his grip fierce as if he was holding himself back. His eyes blazed with emotion. Mostly fury, I thought, and loathing. Not passion or love or understanding.

Kevin dropped the notebook and papers fluttered everywhere. "Oh dear. I'm so sorry, Your Majesty. I'm so clumsy."

He dropped down beside me and started gathering the papers, still babbling like he was terrified of me yelling at him or some such nonsense.

As he handed me a stack of wrinkled papers to hold, I caught the flash of silver in his hand. An old-fashioned fountain pen gleamed against his palm.

Metal tip.

Sharp enough to draw blood.

I gave him a subtle nod. *Do it.*

Then I turned all my attention on Arthur. I tried to smile, but my lips trembled. Hopefully he thought that was overwhelming hope. "Do you really mean it?"

"Of course. I'd do anything for you, my dear. I love you. I always have."

He reached out and touched my knee, thankfully covered by my skirt, but I still shuddered. Revulsion crawled through me. I had to grit my teeth to keep from flinching and shrinking away.

"All I ask is that you never touch him when I'm not there. I'll share, but I want to be involved in everything. That's not too much to ask, is it?"

It *was* too much to ask. I was the fucking queen. I would protect this tower with my Blood and cement the siblings to House Isador. I provided the power. The blood. The heart.

He might be a king, but he'd never form his own goddess-blessed nest. He'd never taste my power or enjoy my pleasure, because I'd rather jab Kevin's trusty pen into my jugular than ever touch Arthur again. If I tried to get through sex with him...

Memories flashed through my mind again, crippling me. Stunning me as surely as a taser. I remembered lying beneath this man as he thrust inside me. Feeling nothing but hatred and disgust.

For myself. Because I was allowing him to have me again, even though I didn't want him. Even though I loved another man.

I'd married Arthur, and he took his marital rights very seriously.

Sobbing in the night. Curled up in a ball. Hating myself. Night after night.

It had never happened to me, but those memories were etched in my soul. I pushed those horrible memories away with effort. Guinevere was sadly not unique in her situation. There were plenty of women who'd been legally bound to men and forced to service them, with no end or hope in sight. I wouldn't go back to that kind of life. I refused to even consider it. Even if that meant Arthur tore Lance limb from limb and made me watch while he ate him.

I. Refused. To fuck Arthur. Ever again.

Period.

"I'm so sorry, Your Majesty," Kevin whispered, pushing closer to me as he reached under my legs. "Some of the papers went under your chair. Forgive me."

He stabbed my calf with the pen.

"Yes," I whispered, allowing my eyes to flare with the pent-up rage boiling inside me. "That *is* too much to ask."

Arthur narrowed a hard look at me, his upper lip curling in disdain as if he'd smelled something nasty. "You forget who I am."

Slowly, I stood. My power rose inside me, fueled by my rage. "No. You forget who *I* am."

He ground his teeth and released a low threatening growl. "You know what I'm capable of. It's too late. I'm already inside the Isador blood circle. I'll kill every single person in this tower, and their blood will be on your head."

"No. If you kill anyone, that's on you."

"What are you going to do?" He shoved up to his feet in one liquid, smooth lunge meant to make me flinch and cower. "Make *me* leave?"

In our bond, I felt Shara so clearly that she could have been standing at my back. Her other sibling, Mayte, stood beside her. Three queens, united, their power at my fingertips.

Shara was the stronger queen, but she didn't hold back her power from me. In my mind's eye, her power gleamed like opal rainbows. Mayte's power was green and lush like the jungle. My power was pure white light. I was to shine like a brilliant captured star on the darkest night.

I braided our powers together and pushed a blast at Arthur, smacking him in the chest.

He staggered back a step, his eyes widening. But then he chuckled, shaking his head. "My little queen has gotten stronger this time around. Excellent. We'll be invincible together. Camelot will be ours once more, Guinevere."

"Gwen," I gritted out. "I'm not her. I never will be. I only have her blood in my veins and her nightmares in my head."

:*Can you kill him now?*: Shara asked :*What's his weakness?*:

:*I don't know. My light doesn't hurt him. I'm mostly a healer. I can make him bleed, but he'd only laugh and enjoy the hell out of it. We've tried to kill him over the centuries, but he always manages to kill us too. We're doomed to die together.:*

:Not this time.: Mayte said in my head. *:I'm mostly a healer too, but I could concoct a nasty virus or plague. The trick will be not allowing him to infect anyone else.:*

I didn't have a blood bond with her directly, but Shara's bond acted as a bridge for us. In fact, I could feel Shara like a wagon wheel, with hundreds of connections spinning out around us. All the Isador siblings she'd acquired. The Zaniyah siblings. Her Blood. We all flashed and twinkled like fireflies around our beautiful dark queen.

:Let's get him out of the circle before he kills anyone,: Shara said. *:Unless you're afraid he'll turn on your Blood as they arrive.:*

I wanted to throw my head back and wail at the risk, but it was our best move. I had to get him out of the circle to protect the tower. My Blood were well used to fighting him. Lance knew that most likely Arthur would be here lying in wait. He wouldn't be stumbling into a fight unaware. *Goddess, please protect them.*

I shoved power at Arthur again, harder this time. He was prepared for me, but with two queens at my back, he couldn't hold his ground.

Hissing, he started to shift to his dragon. Red scales formed on his cheekbones.

:Seize his dragon,: Shara said calmly, giving me a quick image of how she controlled Leviathan. *:You don't have a bond with him, but with the three of us, I think you'll be able to prevent him from shifting.:*

With our power roaring through me, I could see his dragon hovering inside him, swelling with power as he readied to shift. I looped our braided power around his drag-on's neck, and then held on for dear life.

The red dragon bulged against my hold, hissing and

tearing at my magic. It didn't hurt me, exactly, but I wasn't used to channeling so much power. Sweat trickled between my breasts, and my knees trembled. My system was maxed out, red-lined, and quickly overheating. I wouldn't be able to keep up the stream for long.

With my sibling queens at my back, we pushed and shoved the struggling man across the marble floor.

"You can't do this to me," he raged, fighting the wall of power inexorably pushing him toward the door. "I'm the King of Camelot. The Once and Future King! You're mine, Guinevere. Mine!"

"I belong to no man." I panted, gathering the last of my reserves. "Let alone you."

All my rage. My fear, sorrow, and heartache. The suffering I'd endured thanks to this man. I took it all and shoved him with all my might.

He fell back tumbling through the glass windows, sliding across the sidewalk and out of Shara's blood circle.

With my queen's bond raging inside me, I stepped outside through the shattered window and focused on the shimmering wall protecting the tower. I jabbed the crescent moon into my thumb and allowed my blood to drip onto the circle Shara had laid around her building.

"Arthur Pendragon is revoked from this circle. He shall not pass. None of his blood shall pass. So let it be."

He climbed to his feet, his eyes glittering with malice. He brushed at his once-flawless suit with sharp, jerky movements, his jaws clenched. Glass tinkled to the concrete, and he'd torn a hole in one knee. "You forget what I am. I'll just fly over the circle tonight and feast. I'll tear every single one of your precious siblings apart while you watch."

Inside my head, Shara laughed grimly. :*Leviathan assures me even he couldn't soar high enough to get through my circle. Arthur won't have a chance.*:

"Good luck with that." I kept my chin up, shoulders back, and locked my trembling knees. I refused to show any weakness before him. "The last daughter of Isis laid that blood circle. I think it'll stand up to even you."

A man roared far down the sidewalk on my right. "My queen!"

Lance. Goddess. My heart leaped with joy and terror both. If Arthur killed him...

People gasped and shouted as my knights charged up the sidewalk. Three of them. Tall, strong, proud, once the greatest knights of the Round Table, led by my shining golden-haired knight.

I would recognize Lancelot du Lac anywhere. Even with his hair cut short and spiky. Even dressed in jeans rather than armor. His blue-gray eyes blazed with the kind of love that keeps two souls locked on earth, struggling to find each other generation after generation.

All the endless heartache and sorrows of a thousand years. Countless deaths at Arthur's hands. Yet he came to me with the hope that this time...

Maybe he would reach me, and hold me, just for a moment before he died. That would be enough.

Arthur smiled with an awful, wicked glee. He raised his hands, vicious black claws lengthening on each finger.

I gripped the crescent moon and sliced my palm open. I needed more blood, but I knew from experience that even slitting my own throat wouldn't provide enough power to force him off Lancelot.

Shara surged inside me, pushing so much power into me that I started to sag beneath the weight of it. Someone grabbed me, an arm around my waist, helping me stand, as our queen poured through me. I surrendered to her, letting her work through my body as much as she could. Her power exploded in a geyser and wrapped around Arthur's throat like a mighty fist.

"You cannot kill me, Isis," he growled, tearing at the magic trying to strangle him. "This is not your battle."

Shara's voice came out of my mouth. "Gwenhwyvar Findabair carries my blood, and so she carries Isis's blood as well. If you interfere with her, then it *is* my battle."

He jerked his left hand up in front of his face, and the dragon ring spewed some kind of noxious taint into the air. It dissolved Shara's magical hold on him and he sneered at me, his perfect white teeth sharpening into dragon fangs. Shara's flood of power slowed to a trickle, allowing me to straighten slightly, though now I was worried about her. What the fuck was that black stuff? Had it hurt her in some way?

A crowd of New Yorkers had gathered with their phones out. They would capture him shifting into a dragon in live videos, or worse, murdering my Blood on the sidewalk steps from reaching me. I could hear Lance's pounding footsteps. He was close.

Arthur was too strong. If even Shara couldn't stop him...

A gun went off beside me. My ears roared with the retort.

Arthur flinched and turned with a snarl, focusing on...

I turned my head slowly, stunned to see Kevin standing beside me with a handgun held steadily, ready to fire again. He was the one who'd come to my side and supported me. I was grateful, definitely, but what the fuck did he think he was doing?

A gun wouldn't stop the Once and Future King. Certainly not a single shot.

I heard the unmistakable sound of swords being drawn even over the ringing in my ears. Lance raised a heavy broadsword in both hands over his shoulder as he ran to me. His mouth opened on a wordless shout. He charged into battle as he always did, without thought or concern for himself.

Only me. Protect me. At all cost.

Kevin shot again, striking Arthur in the other shoulder. He jerked to the side with the impact, a grimace on his face. He started to laugh, shaking his head with amusement. But his laughter cut off on a curse.

He rubbed at the spreading blood and hissed. Smoke started to rise up from beneath his suit jacket.

"Silver bullets," Kevin said. "It won't kill him, but it'll hurt like a bitch until he can dig them out."

Arthur glared at us, cast a look around at the throng of onlookers, and whirled on his heel to stride away in the opposite direction.

I sagged with relief against Kevin. "We did it. Goddess above, I didn't think it was possible to hold him off."

My knights slowed as they approached the circle. I read the hesitation in Lance's eyes. He wanted to come to me first, but the warrior in him insisted he go after Arthur while he was wounded and take any advantage we had to try and kill him.

But we'd lived this battle over and over and over. If he went after Arthur now...

He'd die. And then I'd die without him. Like countless times before.

"Lance." I started toward him, my steps unsteady. Kevin kept an arm around my waist, moving with me. I quickened my pace, desperate to reach my knight. To bring him inside the circle. To touch him. Kiss him. Taste him. Running the last few steps, I threw myself into his arms. He clutched me against him and lifted me off my feet.

My body knew him, every fiber and texture of his muscles. His height. His smell. Leather and sandalwood. His tawny hair wasn't as long as Guinevere insisted it should be, but I knew he'd have a gorgeous lion mane when he shifted.

He squeezed me so hard I couldn't breathe. Blindly, I turned my face toward his, unable to see for the tears. I didn't need to see him to find his mouth.

I inhaled his lips, drinking down his groan. His cheeks were rough with stubble. He'd been traveling for days, racing across the globe to find me. Against all odds, he was here. Alive. And I couldn't get enough of him. I stroked the bare skin of his throat and hunger blazed in me.

His blood would undo me.

I'd never wanted anything more in my life.

He released my lips so he could press his forehead to mine. His breath panted across my face, his body shuddering against me. "My queen. My love."

"Come inside," I whispered, stroking the beloved planes of his face. "I need to know you're safe."

One of the other men stepped up and took his sword so he could more easily hold me.

"Bors," I cried, reaching for him. "You made it."

He looked more like a tattooed motorcycle club member than a former knight, and I loved it. He stepped up close and wrapped both me and Lance in his arms. "My queen, I kept him alive as long as I could, hoping you'd be able to call us."

I kissed the scar on his forehead. "Thank you, my love." Blinking away the first happy tears of my entire life, I met my third Blood's shimmering honey-amber eyes. "Oh, Mordred. Thank the goddess you made it too." I untwined my arm from Lance's neck so I could reach out for him. Mordred took my hand as Lance carried me across the blood circle, while I touched the other two knights.

Inside Shara's circle, they'd be safer, at least. Though the battle was far from over.

"That's all for today, folks," Kevin said loudly to the

onlookers. "I hope you enjoyed the show. Come back again next week!"

I didn't think the crowd would buy it, but I didn't really care. Closing my eyes, I pressed my face to Lance's throat and just breathed. So good. I wanted to wallow in his scent and cement our bond immediately, but first, I reached out to Shara.

:Are you okay? What did Arthur do to you?:

She didn't answer right away, which made my heart rate quicken with dread. I tightened my focus on our bond, reaching toward her. If she needed healing…

:I'm fine,: she finally answered, her bond steady and sure, though thinner, as if she'd taken a hit and needed to conserve her strength. *:Where did that ring come from?:*

:Guinevere gave it to him on their wedding day.:

:That's the key to his power and the curse. There's something very malevolent tied to it. It drained my power like a leech before I could disconnect from it. So now it'll be even stronger.:

:Great.: I sighed internally. *:I'll see if I can find out more about it and where it came from.:*

:That ring sustains and protects him. Take it, destroy it, and I believe the curse will end.:

She sounded tired and achy. In our bond, I felt her Blood gathered close, soothing her with touch and blood. Guilt twinged. We couldn't risk damaging Shara, or we'd all die. She was our queen and protected us all.

:I'm tired, not hurt,: she replied tartly, giving me a gentle mental shake. *:We held him off, so this was a victory, not a defeat. Take your Blood. Celebrate. Then we'll come up with the final battle plan to end this for good.:*

Take my Blood.

Goddess above, when had Guinevere ever actually lived long enough to taste Lancelot's blood again? Meanwhile, here he stood, holding me in his arms on the sidewalk in front of the tower.

"Kevin, can you take care of replacing the glass? And deal with whatever media questions come up?"

Grinning, he pulled open the door and Lance swept through with my other two Blood on his heels. "Replacement glass has already been ordered. I'll hold all questions until tomorrow morning, but if anything urgent arises, I'll call Gina."

"Thank you, Kevin. Without your help…"

He inclined his head, a very old-fashioned gesture that fit him well despite his youth. "My pleasure, Your Majesty."

5

LANCE

I clutched my queen in my arms and fought the urge to run. I'd carry her away to the furthest, most forlorn place in the Gibson Desert I could find. We'd hide from Arthur and the world at large. I'd keep her safe. No one would ever harm her again.

But even in my wildest fantasies, I knew it could never be.

Her Majesty Guinevere Findabair, the White Enchantress, had never fled from her duties. The queen of Camelot had many responsibilities. She cared for all the people in her house, whether it was this modern skyscraper or the fabled castle of old. She'd never abandon those under her care, even to keep herself safe.

Arthur knew that. Which was exactly how he'd been able to find and kill her over and over again.

"Put me down, Lance."

I did so at once, even though it felt as though letting go of her tore my own skin off my body. These eyes had never seen her before, yet I would know her anywhere. She had the same lustrous mahogany hair, though she wore it in a single

braid rather than coiled around her head. Her changeable
hazel eyes saw everything laid bare at a glance.

Guinevere of old had been a small, delicate woman. This
lifetime, she was taller, almost to my shoulder, and not nearly
as ethereal though every bit as beautiful as I remembered.
She wore a bright red dress with large white stripes and full
skirt that swung about her knees. I'd never paid much attention to women's fashion, but I hadn't seen anyone dressed
like this. It reminded me of a style worn in black-and-white
movies decades ago.

The matching red heels she wore made her legs go on
forever. Guinevere would have adored those shoes, too.
She'd loved bright, unexpected colors. She'd never been
allowed to wear—

My thoughts died off, my brain locking down.

White and red stripes.

Sir Lancelot du Lac's coat of arms.

She paused, sensing the turbulent emotions tearing
through me. Smiling over her shoulder, she took my hand
and gave me a little tug until I started moving again.

"I'm Gwen in this lifetime." She led us onto an elevator
and pressed the button for the top floor. "This tower isn't
mine, but I hold it for my queen, Shara Isador, last daughter
of Isis. She made me her sibling a few days ago, and that's
what broke Elaine's hold on me."

Hearing that name on my queen's lips made my shoulders
tense. As if Arthur wasn't enough, Elaine was still alive too.
Fucking great. No guesses where Arthur was headed this
very moment. He'd regroup with Elaine and kill us when we
went after Merlin. Again.

Bors cleared his throat roughly. "Is that why you couldn't
call us, my queen?"

"Yes. She made me swear never to call my Blood."
Squeezing my hand, she leaned against me, and it shamed me

to realize she was trying to protect me. To make me feel better.

Because yeah, that woman's name still made my stomach queasy, and I hadn't even encountered her in this lifetime.

"I won't let her have you," Gwen whispered fiercely. "You're mine, Lancelot du Lac. You're my alpha. My Blood. My love. Nothing will take you from me this time. I swear it."

"I love you more than my life, as you well know, my queen. But please, don't make promises that we can't keep."

She straightened, her chin tipping up at a haughty angle that made pride roar in my heart. Her cheekbones were stark and proud, her lips lush but firm, her face so fucking regal. This was my queen. The queen of the ages. Forget King Arthur. The poems and idylls should have been dedicated to her. The Once and Always Queen of my heart.

"I fully intend to keep this promise, sir knight. I have many advantages in this lifetime that have never been available to us before. I'm older, for one. Elaine's geas may have kept us apart, but it also kept us alive. I've dedicated that time to improving myself and my abilities as much as possible despite not having any Blood of my own. Now, I have a queen sibling who's powerful enough to control this entire continent. With her help, I held off Arthur so that you could enter the circle. He didn't kill you on sight. When has that ever happened before?"

"Never," Mordred muttered darkly. "But we all know what his next step will be, and it's an insurmountable obstacle."

The elevator doors opened, and our queen started to step outside. Bors managed to slip past her first, while Mordred stepped up to block her exit. I expected her to be irritated at our interference, but she leaned back against me and slipped her arms around my waist.

"I forgot what it's like to have protection. Thank you, my Blood."

"Clear," Bors called.

Only then did Mordred step aside, bowing as our queen passed. Bors stood several paces away, scanning back and forth between two doors, waiting for any threat to arise. She stepped to the door on the left, and he immediately took up position, waiting on her to unlock it so he could search the premises.

"This entire building is warded and protected by the Isador blood circle," Gwen said. "Nothing could possibly harm me now."

"Arthur was inside the circle," I reminded her.

She scowled and heaved out a sigh. "True. But that was not my doing. He'd been allowed in by the previous Skye queen."

"Who else could she have allowed inside? For all we know, Elaine Shalott could have been granted access."

Gwen shook her head emphatically. "That I can attest against with one-hundred-percent confidence. No one of House Shalott is inside this circle."

Except my queen. She carried Elaine's blood. That was a new wrinkle in this lifetime. Would Elaine know the moment Gwen claimed me? Would she feel the surge in my queen's power? The pleasure?

Because I'd fucking kill myself pleasuring our queen.

Gwen's eyes smoldered, changing from a blue-green hazel to mossy green. Turning, she casually walked over to the massive bed centered in the room. Heavy wooden posts rose from the corners to hold aloft a ten-foot-tall frame swathed with white gauzy streamers. Pausing, she looked back over her shoulder at me, curling her right hand around behind to slowly unzip her dress.

The sound was loud in the room, the silence broken only

by the heavy breathing of three enraptured men as the dress slowly fell off her glorious body.

I would have thought she was beautiful whether she was thin or curvy, short or tall. I'd loved her many bodies over the centuries—if given the privilege to see her, even from afar—drawn by her inner spirit more than her physical beauty. But I had to admit that this body had been carved with exquisite perfection by the goddesses.

I traced the lines of her shoulders, proud and strong yet still feminine, down the curve of her spine, the dip of her waist, the swell of her buttocks and hips, to the gentle curve of her calves. A small trickle of dried blood held my gaze a moment, before I dragged my gaze back up for another long drink of her body.

She wore thin white lacy scraps that enhanced the mounds of her ass and breasts as she slowly turned to face me. Her power hummed in the air, glowing from her skin as if she was lit from within by the full silvered moon. Even her skin was flawless, creamy silk.

"How many lifetimes have we never even laid eyes on each other? Let alone been in the same room together."

I swallowed the razor blades in my throat. "Too many to count."

"How many lifetimes have you tasted my blood and carried my bond?"

"Never enough," I rasped out, fisting my hands at my sides. Overwhelming thirst licked through my veins, driving me to madness. I hadn't tasted Aima blood in years. Never a queen's blood in the four hundred years I'd been alive. Let alone *Guinevere's* blood...

I had no idea how long it'd been since Lancelot du Lac had fed from his queen and given his life's blood to strengthen her in return. The memories of doom that were written in my soul insisted it had been millennia.

Muscles clenched, I fought to keep my position until she said otherwise. "A handful at most."

Sitting on the edge of the bed, she reached down to slip off the red heels one by one. "We should do something about that, then." She glanced up at me through her lashes and laughed softly. "All of you."

I don't remember moving a muscle, let alone crossing the ten paces or more to her side, but suddenly I was on my knees before her with my brothers-in-arms on either side of me. "My queen. We're yours. Use us as you see fit."

6

GWEN

I cupped Lance's cheek and smoothed my thumb over his mouth. He trembled beneath the slight touch, but he made no move to touch me. No Blood would ever touch his queen unless invited. He certainly wouldn't feed until my thirst was met. It had nothing to do with chivalry, but a Blood's complete dedication to his queen.

He would always put my needs before his. My safety before his. Especially as my alpha.

Goddess, it hurt my heart to look at him, aching with need, his lips parted to make room for his fangs so he didn't puncture his own lips or tongue. I didn't need a full bond to know how much those long ivories were throbbing, because mine sent a constant throb deep into my skull.

Staring into his eyes, I felt as though I should say something to mark this momentous occasion. The greatest knight of the Round Table had survived over four hundred years despite our enemies' schemes to find me once again, as he'd served countless times before. Even knowing that he would most likely die horribly.

It wasn't our fate to go gently into the darkness, but raging and spitting curses at our enemies.

Memories of past lives fluttered in my mind, pages of a book that had no end. Betrayal. Shocking horror. Pain. Aching loneliness. Misery.

Staring at each other across a room, unable to touch. Unable to speak.

Or worse, holding his head in my lap as the light died in his eyes and blood dripped from his wounds.

Rage swirled inside me like a devastating hurricane, tearing that awful book to shreds. Papers flapped and tore away one by one, leaving only a tattered spine of the book I'd come to hate so much.

No more pages of agony and heartache and despair. This time...

I would write us a new book. A future where we could be together. Forever.

I started to lean down to his throat, intending to be gentle. To honor him with a graceful bite, this legendary knight of beauty and skill. But the warmth of his skin beckoned, his scent filling my nose. Warm sandalwood and well-used leather, like a favorite saddle that had been polished and oiled for decades because of its perfect fit.

He was perfect. He was here. And I couldn't contain my thirst any longer.

I struck hard, sinking my fangs deeply into his neck, tearing through his carotid artery. So much blood, surging into my mouth eagerly before I could even retract my fangs.

I gasped against his throat, clutching him. He tasted exactly like his personality, as if his blood carried timeless love, shining honor, and pure, sweet silver.

Goddess. So long.

Just as I'd known him on sight, my power knew him and reveled in his blood.

Guinevere had been the White Enchantress, a famed witch queen with a thirst for blood, at least to those who knew the true history. She'd worked her magic to protect her knights, care for her people, and heal the sick, but she'd also worked the darker magics to ensure the best crops, performed the fertility rites, and created charms to protect against the fae creatures that preyed upon our kind as well as humans.

All of which had involved sacrifice.

Blood sacrifice.

Usually her own, but her knights had willingly bled for her too. Her power had been immense, something I couldn't even comprehend until I'd met Shara Isador. Surely my new queen came close to the power that Guinevere had wielded so effortlessly.

She had great magic, yes, but that magic was powered by her Blood. She'd drawn on Sir Lancelot's blood to build Camelot. She'd used Merlin's to ward her knights. Bors, Mordred, and yes, even Arthur, had flavored her power and the magic she worked, and she'd used that power to protect them all.

I'd never had that kind of power.

Until now.

Lance's blood surged through me like wildfire. Cells that had lain dormant my entire life suddenly stirred. Barren fields, blasted into a desert by a lifetime of drought, sparked with new life. Riverbeds long dry, now dampening with a trickle. A stream. Then a torrent of crashing waters that flooded through me.

So much power.

I locked my arms and legs around him. I lifted my mouth only long enough to say, "I want you inside me," and then sealed my mouth back over my mark so I could drink my fill.

He let out a rough growl and pushed up from his knees to

slam me on my back onto the mattress. He jerked at my panties, silk tearing in his haste to complete my order. I didn't release his throat as he started to push inside me, but I groaned with bliss. He slid into me on one long, slow glide all the way to the hilt. Then he lay against me, giving me his full weight.

As I'd always liked, even as Gwen in this lifetime.

Crying, I held him with my entire body. Squeezing him tightly, inside and out. So long. I couldn't even remember the last lifetime that he'd been both my Blood and my lover.

I wanted to drink from him until we both passed out in bliss, but I also wanted so much more than his blood. He didn't move or thrust, even though he felt like a steel sword inside me. I ran my hands down his shoulders and back, and his muscles quivered. My Blood was on the edge of release, without moving an inch inside me.

I licked my jagged punctures and dropped my head back to the pillow so I could see his face.

His eyes burned with lust. Sweat trickled down his forehead, his nostrils flaring with each labored breath. But he waited for my next order.

I cupped his cheek and rubbed my thumb over his parted lips. His fangs glistened like small swords, so long and brutal it made me shiver to remember the feel of him inside me.

Dick and fangs, piercing me. It had been so fucking long.

Yet he waited, determined to carry out my every wish before indulging in his own needs. He'd never understood that I loved watching him come inside me as much as any pleasure he could give me.

I didn't say anything, but only turned my face aside to bare my throat.

He shuddered, his dick thumping hard inside me, lengthening even more.

As if in slow motion, he lowered his head. My hips automatically tipped up, taking him deeper. Because I knew that when he sank his fangs into me...

I was going to come. Hard.

He knew it too.

With exquisite care, he pierced my throat. I felt the slide of his fangs inside me, a mini thrust, even though his hips didn't move. My clit pulsed, and I came apart beneath him. Power crashed and rolled inside me, thrusting me up into the stratosphere only to slam me back to earth. I clawed at his back and writhed beneath him, every muscle begging for him to move. I wanted him thrusting into me. Pinning me. Sweat and muscle straining to please me. Out of control.

"Lance!"

The sound of his name on my lips had always been his undoing. He slid one hand beneath my neck, cradling my head so he didn't accidentally tear his punctures. I felt his other hand sliding up past my head to grip one of the headboard bars for leverage.

Then he flexed, as if his body was one giant muscle. His back heaved, his buttocks tightening beneath my hands. I dug my fingers into his ass, urging him harder. Deeper. He still hadn't let go. Not completely.

I had a sudden horrible thought. I hadn't asked him if Elaine had gotten to him in this lifetime. If she'd taken him, and hurt him or forced him...

:*No,*: he growled in my mind. :*I'm yours. Only yours.*:

His mind touched mine and I could cry at how beautiful it felt to have him inside me, body and heart and soul. At last. *At last.*

My blood stirred his beast, the manticore. If his lion didn't tear you apart, you'd die from his poisonous scorpion tail. Plus, he could fly, his leathery wings more like a dragon than a bird's. Against most enemies, the manticore would have been a formidable, unbeatable opponent.

But Arthur's massive dragon had always dwarfed him. I couldn't bear watching the dragon tear Lance's manticore apart again like a giant bird of prey playing with its food.

With my bond taking root in Lance, I felt his release boiling up his spine, ready to erupt. He threw his head back, dribbling my blood down his chin. He pulled back, almost withdrawing completely, so he could slam back inside me. My breath rushed out on a low grunt. There, that was the delicious, heavy throb I wanted to feel. He thrust again, thudding up inside me so hard that I saw stars. Brilliant white starbursts that spun through my head. Brighter. Until a blast of white completely overwhelmed my senses.

Shuddering with release, I clung to him as he shook and strained on top of me. His breath rushed out on a deep bellow that rattled his chest against me. He spurted inside me, a hot flood of desire that my body lapped up as eagerly as his blood.

Breathing hard, he collapsed on top of me, his body twitching as he came down from the rush of pleasure and the high of my blood. He tried to lift his head, but even that was too much effort.

"Shhh," I whispered, cradling his head against my throat.

"You need," he panted, "to take them too."

I lifted my right hand toward the side of the bed, and immediately Bors wrapped his fingers around mine and came onto the mattress with us. "I will. But you don't have to move far."

Effortlessly, Bors helped me shift Lance off to my opposite side. Close enough to still cuddle against me but giving me room to pull Bors down into my arms too. I took a moment to study the tattoos inked across his upper body. Swords, shields, roses, and skulls wove an intricate design across his chest. Above his heart, he'd inked *my queen*.

I loved that he hadn't tattooed *Guinevere* on his chest,

since that wasn't *my* name, but he'd still marked himself as belonging to me.

Leaning up, I pressed my lips to those words.

"I left room to have your name inked below it as soon as you called me."

I breathed his scent, lightly rubbing my lips back and forth against his skin. Crushed spruce needles, as if a large animal had silently passed in a dark, primordial forest. Since he transformed into a giant stag, that made perfect sense. "I love it. I bet you ride a motorcycle too."

He smiled against my temple. "Naturally. There aren't any warhorses in this day and age, so a Harley is the next best thing."

I tipped my head back so I could see his face. I trailed my fingers over the long scar on his forehead. Funny how he always ended up with that scar through the ages, though the cause was different each lifetime. "A motorcycle accident?"

Lance had recovered enough to snort. "Hardly. It was a bar fight in Dublin if I remember correctly, though we were both pretty drunk."

For Aima to be drunk enough that he couldn't remember exactly where it'd been... "Did you put away an entire keg?"

"Nearly," Bors replied. "But it wasn't humans we got into a fight with. Some of *her* Blood were there, looking for Lance. They tried to take him."

"Idiots," he muttered. "We had to kill them. They wouldn't leave empty handed."

"After that, we decided to stick to the uninhabited places in the world until you could call us."

"We also stayed apart as long as possible," Lance added. "It was safer that way. We figured we'd double our chances that at least one of us could get to you."

Oh, goddess. The thought of them each living alone for all these centuries...

Granted, I'd been alone too, but Lance and Bors had always been lovers. They could have at least had each other for company until I was able to call them. Blinking back fresh tears, I slid my hand up around Bors' nape and pulled him down closer. "So we have a lot of lost time to make up for, don't we?"

He made a low, welcoming growl of approval as I sank my fangs into his throat. His blood filled my mouth, and the first swallow carried a punch to my gut like potent, aged wine. Deep and dark and still like that ancient forest, magical and untouched by humanity. The kind of place where the Wild Hunt still roamed at night.

His stag filled my mind, an ancient, proud white deer standing on a craggy mountain, as big as a moose, with huge, sweeping antlers like thick trees. He turned his magnificent head toward me and slowly started to bow.

No. He should never bow to me. None of my knights should ever bow, not when they sacrificed everything to keep me alive. I couldn't tell him through the bond yet, since he hadn't had my blood, but he knew me well enough to know without the words.

"I will always bow to you, my queen. I'll go down on my knees every single day and praise our goddesses that you lived another day to grace this cruel world with your presence."

Lance shifted away from me, leaving my side cold for a second. But then Mordred slid in beside me, pressing me tighter to Bors.

Two magnificent men holding me. A third man who loved me enough to step aside and make space for the others that I loved, without making a single demand on me. Arthur had never been able to make room for others around us.

"Don't think of him," Mordred whispered, stroking my arm soothingly. I hadn't realized I'd tensed up until I relaxed between them. He didn't need a blood bond with me to know the only person I'd ever tense up about was the king who believed he had the sole, rightful claim on my heart.

I wanted to block out those memories that weren't even mine. I wanted to imprint my Blood on every inch of my body. Only they would ever touch me. Only they would ever feel my pleasure and my love.

Only them. Forever.

I hooked my thigh over Bors' hips, opening myself to him as I wriggled closer. He reached between us and adjusted himself so I could take him inside me. So good, to have my knights pressed tightly against me, front and back. But I wanted Mordred inside me too.

I didn't have to tell them. They knew me inside and out, even though we'd only just met face to face. No matter how many times we'd lived and died, one truth always remained.

This. My knights. Giving me their blood, their bodies, their love.

I smelled Mordred's blood, the sweet, thick scent of honey that I recognized deep down in Guinevere's memories. My golden eagle. He stroked bloody fingers down my crack to provide lubrication, but he didn't stop there. He smeared his blood on Bors' dick too, so that each of his slow thrusts carried Mordred's blood inside me.

I swore I could feel it burning deep inside my core. I groaned against Bors' throat, tightening my grip on him. I wanted them both inside me. I needed it. I needed to feel that connection with them. Their blood mingling with mine, as well as their semen seeping into me.

My power hungered for their release.

"She wants you to hurry, asshole," Bors growled to the other knight, his voice tight with strain as he held back his desire.

Mordred smiled against my ear. "Oh? Is that true, my

queen? I thought I'd just watch Bors for a while. He's so pretty when he's sweating and groaning to please you."

In answer, I bumped my ass back against him demandingly, even though that meant I almost lost Bors inside me.

Mordred took the hint and slowly pressed inside me, taking his time so I could adjust. Oh fuck, it'd been a long time since I'd had two Blood at once. Never in this lifetime. While Guinevere remembered taking her Blood like this many times, it was a new sensation for me. Stretching, burning, it was almost too much. But Mordred was in no hurry. How, I had no idea. Urgency hammered inside me, even though I'd already had Lance. I wanted their release too. Desperately.

Yet Mordred didn't rush me. Finally, my muscles loosened enough to let him slide balls deep in my ass. Bors pressed closer. Filling me completely. Pressure built inside me. I couldn't lie still, not with so much dick inside me. Trembling, I shifted between them, which stirred a fresh wave of nerve endings.

I had to release Bors' throat so I could breath and not choke myself on blood every time I gasped. Pressing my wrist to his mouth, I arched my neck to the side for Mordred.

Two sets of fangs pierced me. Two dicks stuffed inside me. Orgasm surged through me in a sudden wave that made me scream. Searing white power flooded me, pushing me higher. A blazing supernova, shining, pure light that could never be denied. This was the kind of power that rocked the foundations of the world and drove back all the demonic creatures preying in the night.

Even a vicious, undefeated dragon. Goddess, I hoped so.

My release pushed Bors over the edge. He bucked against me, driving me back more fully on Mordred's cock. Gripping my throat in his mouth, Mordred flooded into me in a hot wave.

Panting, I slowly came back to awareness. Bors and Mordred both still fed on my blood. I didn't feel drained or weakened, so Lance wasn't worried about how much they were taking. Yet.

Tears burned in my eyes. My Blood. I could feel their bonds inside me, swelling and growing with power. The more blood they took, the stronger they would be. The more blood I took, the tighter our bond.

As soon as I thought it, Mordred wrapped his right arm around me and pressed his wrist to my lips. A not-so-subtle reminder that I hadn't fed on him yet.

I sank my fangs in the tender flesh of his inner wrist, and his dick stirred to life against my buttocks. I made a low rumbling hum of hunger, both from the sweet taste of his blood and his desire. I'd make full use of them both, as many times as we could. Over and over and over.

I had almost four-hundred years of loneliness to make up for, and thousands of years of a miserable curse to break. They'd be hard pressed to find a moment where I didn't have fangs or their dicks inside me. Preferably both.

All three of my Blood said in my head, :*Sounds good to me.*:

7

GWEN

W e'd done it. We'd finally lived long enough to find each other.

Lance and Mordred lay on either side of me, cuddling me between them. Bors lay deeper in the bed, wedged in on Lance's side between our legs, his face pressed against my hip, his arm draped over my thighs.

"This is quite the nest you've claimed, my queen," Mordred said. "How many stories is this tower?"

"One hundred, but it's not mine. I merely hold it for House Isador." I stroked my fingers over Bors' buzz cut, enjoying the feel of the short hair against my skin. "It's no Camelot."

Lance hummed against my throat. "It's better."

I lifted my head so I could see his eyes. "Guinevere built those shining walls with her own blood. That's why the legend persists, despite the way Arthur spoiled everything with his curse. Nothing will ever shine like Camelot ever again."

"Camelot was never about the castle, my queen. It was always you."

"I built nothing here." Until I said the words, I didn't realize that it bothered me. I was thankful to be alive. I was extremely grateful to Shara for everything she'd done for me, including making me her sibling. If she hadn't been at my back today...

I wouldn't have been able to hold Arthur off.

My knights would be dead before I could claim them. Instead of making love with my Blood, I'd have been fucked by the king. Or I would have been dead. I knew which I would prefer if given the choice.

However, I hated feeling like a squatter. While I'd added my blood to the protective circle around the building, it was only to affirm my relationship with the primary queen. It was *her* circle. Her nest.

It would never be *my* Camelot.

"It doesn't matter." Lance's eyes flashed with fierce pride that surprised me, even as it brought tears to my eyes. "Nothing matters but you. You survived. You called us. You've taken Blood for the first time in centuries. You even escaped Arthur—"

"For the time being," I broke in. "You know he'll be back."

"Yes. He will. He can't resist the call of Camelot, either."

"He can't resist *your* call," Mordred whispered, tucking my shoulder back beneath his chin. "Especially now that you've called your power. You've taken Camelot, my queen. The power is yours. The White Enchantress lives again. When has that happened in the last thousand years?"

I blew out a slow breath, my mind whirling. They were right. I didn't think Guinevere's line had been able to embrace her power in several generations. Certainly, never as fully as the original queen of Camelot. Arthur's jealous curse and Elaine's desperate plots to steal Lance away from me always destroyed Camelot before it could ever rise.

Before I could take my power.

Silvery white power ebbed and flowed inside me. A captured star shining in my heart.

Lance placed his palm over my heart. "This is Camelot, my queen. What the Once and Future King covets most of all."

My face hardened. The soft, shining light inside me crystalized into a diamond's cutting edge. "Then this time, he'll be the Once and *Dead* King."

8

GWEN

I t felt incredible to be free of Elaine Shalott. After over three hundred years, she had no blood hold on me. My mind and power were my own.

Lance was mine. I'd called him and two others of my Blood despite the wretched oath she'd made me swear as a thirteen-year-old girl.

She'd failed... but the war between Houses Camelot and Shalott was far from over. She still guarded the entrance to the legendary island, Avalon—where my cantankerous wizard had been imprisoned for well over a thousand years.

Some stories claimed that a mortally wounded King Arthur had been carried away from the battlefield by three women in a boat to heal and rest on Avalon. One day, he'd return and save the world when it needed him again.

Disgust curled my upper lip at the thought. Arthur had certainly returned, over and over and over. Never to save the world, but to destroy Guinevere's ancient and powerful house. Only my aunt and I still carried a bit of Queen Guinevere's blood. If I failed to break his curse this time, I didn't

think a trace of her would ever be reborn to try again. Arthur
—and ultimately Elaine—would win.

Merlin would be trapped for all time. Lance and the rest
of my Blood would never have the peace for which their
souls had fought for generations. Not if their queen was dead
and lost forever.

I had to find a way to stop Arthur once and for all. Which
meant I had to free Merlin.

Even if that meant knocking on Elaine's back door.

The legends varied about Avalon's location, but Glastonbury Tor had long been associated with the mystical isle.
Centuries ago, the ancient hill had been surrounded by
marshes, making it a popular guess for the island's location.
The tor was important, but only because of the Chalice Well.

When my aunt had agreed to swear allegiance to Shalott
in exchange for my life, Elaine had taken me to the well to
formalize the sibling exchange of blood. Then she'd gleefully
told me that we stood by the portal to Avalon—but I would
never be allowed to use it. I was never allowed to call any of
my own Blood, but especially Merlin would be lost to me.

Forever.

Deliberate torture, even though I was only a child. So
close, but so far away.

The Chalice Well was a public site, but she'd laid a special
blood circle around it to alert her if I came anywhere near it.
I'd felt that warning's energy lifting my hair and crackling
along my skin. She'd know immediately if I stepped foot
anywhere near the beautiful garden surrounding the well.

We'd danced back and forth in this grim battle for far too
long for her not to know every possible step I might take. So
I had to surprise her. Somehow.

If the Chalice Well was off limits...

Maybe there was another way to reach Avalon. Though
when I asked my knights, my beloved alpha frowned doubt-

60 JOELY SUE BURKHART

fully. "I've never heard of any other location or site associated with Avalon that carries the same power as Glastonbury Tor, my queen."

My three Blood might have been reborn knights of the Round Table, but they'd fully embraced the modern age in which we now lived. Mordred had taken over a small room just off my bedchamber and installed several computers and monitors. I didn't even know when he'd had time to find all the equipment, let alone set it up, but none of it had been there when I'd taken Lance and Kevin through the heart tree in the basement to Shara Isador's nest. We'd only been gone an hour at most to formalize Kevin's oath as Shara's second consiliarius.

Spinning his chair away from the monitors to face me, Mordred grinned. "I work quickly, my queen."

"So I see. What's all this for?"

Bors grunted as he leaned back against the wall by the door. "Goddess, here we go. Time for a technology lesson."

Mordred's golden eyes gleamed with mischievous anticipation, a light that drew me inexorably closer. I curled my hand around his neck, stroking my fingertips over his tight curls. "Actually, I'm prepared to give a mythology and history lesson."

Bors sighed dramatically. "Even better. Maybe I should go patrol the tower instead."

I didn't heave a sigh, but I wasn't too eager for a long lecture either. My nerves were drawn tight, simmering with pent-up magic. Every cell in my body screamed with urgency. I had to get Merlin. Now. I needed to act. I needed to make a move before Elaine checkmated me.

But if I'd learned anything in the last few decades serving my former queen, Keisha Skye, it was the importance of the long game. She'd been willing to set a geas on House Zaniyah and wait forty years for their queen to fall. Shara Isador's mother had been an even greater master of the game, moving pieces across the board more than a century before she'd been ready to deliver her heir and disappear without a trace to protect her.

I couldn't afford a single mistake. Not in this game. Like it or not, Elaine had started this war nearly four hundred years ago when she'd gained my aunt's allegiance. I'd managed to stay alive, and Lance had stayed free, against all odds. I couldn't throw all that away on a knee-jerk move that would get us all killed.

Lance stepped out of the room a moment, surprising me. Until he returned with one of the padded chairs for me to sit in. Evidently this really was going to be a lengthy discussion. I sat down facing Mordred, and Lance's hand settled on my right shoulder. A phantom memory flickered through me. One of Guinevere's memories, not mine, but incredibly real.

The pleasant weight of his bare hand on my shoulder. The faintest brush of his finger on the bare skin of my throat. A quick, indulgent stroke in open court while our lord and my husband, King Arthur, argued with a group of ambassadors. It had been such a small touch, certainly nothing to remark about. He hadn't groped me blatantly or acted disrespectful in any way.

Yet Arthur had seen that tender touch that spoke of intimacy and yearning. His eyes had narrowed into burning slits, revealing the rabid dragon smoldering inside him.

:*He couldn't bear to share one moment of your love.*: Even in our bond, Lance's voice broke with sorrow. :*Even if that meant destroying us all.*:

I reached up and closed my fingers around his, both to make sure he didn't withdraw, and also to openly affirm and welcome his touch. Even here, in complete privacy in my quarters, I felt centuries of lingering formality and chivalry that had been bred into his very bones.

My knight put my safety first. Always.

A guard was no guard if he was too busy loving his queen to be aware of approaching danger. He'd fought against betraying our love for far too long to indulge in open affection like this—unless I made sure to encourage it.

:*All my love is yours,*: I replied in our bond, making sure to radiate those thoughts to all of my Blood. :*We have no need to hide our love any longer, my knights.*:

I gave a nod to Mordred to continue his lesson.

"I've made use of these past centuries, my queen. With computers such as these, containing vast databases and libraries more massive than anything Merlin himself could have ever acquired, I've researched Avalon and your history, hoping to find a way to help you break the curse."

I leaned forward slightly, hope stirring in my heart. "And?"

"You need a way to Avalon that doesn't alert *her* of your presence, right? What if I tell you that I don't believe Merlin is in Avalon at all? Or at the very least, he's locked beyond our world in a more encompassing place than a singular island."

"But he is in Avalon. She told me so. Standing at the edge of that well, I could feel something beyond the water, as if it was just a thin veil separating our world from beyond."

Mordred nodded eagerly. "Exactly. That veil is mentioned over and over in all of the ancient legends. 'Beyond the veil' could mean many things. Avalon, certainly, but it could also refer to the generic Otherworld. There are many such parallel universes described in the ancient legends. I've read every treatise on Arthurian literature from Tennyson to Chrétien de Troyes and even back to Geoffrey of Monmouth. Over the years, many stories have changed to reflect the times in which they were told, but there's a fairytale aspect to them that never changes. For example, who supposedly made Excalibur? Who raised Lancelot du Lac?"

"Morgan." Lance replied. "Or sometimes a more generic Lady of the Lake, but it's not clear if they're the same woman. No one ever really knew who Morgan was."

"Morgan *le Fay*," Mordred said. "The fairy. Some stories even described her as more of a goddess. Some say she was Arthur's elder stepsister, but that she was supernatural in some way. Others say she was an enchantress. But the name implies something magical. Otherworldly.

"Which led me exploring other tales. Did you know that the Tuatha dé Danann—Irish fairies—were also descended from gods and goddesses, much the same as we Aima are? Their Otherworld, Tír na nÓg, is also an island. The Welsh underworld is another mystical island, Annwn. There are so many similarities and overlaps between Celtic and Irish folklore and Arthurian stories. Maybe the lines were blurred for a reason."

It actually made a strange kind of sense. The only bedtime stories older than vampires were fairy tales. "So you think all of these mystical islands are actually the same place, just different names?"

"Exactly, and each name is associated with different passageways. Sometimes it was a fairy mound. For other cultures, it was a burial mound. Some still believe that Stonehenge might have been some kind of portal to the Otherworld. The names of the Otherworld might have differed, but the ways to them always involved some kind of portal that pierced the veil between the worlds."

The word *ways* kept echoing in my head. Maybe because I had just returned through Shara's heart tree in the basement. In a few steps, I'd gone from her tower here in New York City to Eureka Springs and then back again. The actual passage had taken less than five minutes.

She'd told me that I would be able to travel to England much the same way, though the portals might not be trees for me. The new tree in the basement could take me to Eureka Springs, or England, or anywhere.

So why not Avalon?

It took all my will not to leap to my feet, race to the elevator, and test out this new theory. I was afraid to embrace the flutter of hope in my chest—for fear it would wither and die. I couldn't even voice the idea, though my Blood had picked up on it in our bond.

"Forgive me, my queen." Lance squeezed my shoulder gently. "But I suspect even the Isador heart tree won't access Avalon directly."

"He's right," Mordred said. "A physical object like a tree that's rooted deeply in the soil would likely only access the earthly plane itself, unless you gained a new power that would allow you to pierce the veil to the Otherworld directly. If the Chalice Well is truly a portal to Avalon, then I would suspect other watery portals might exist that involve a passage through to the non-earthly plane. That's why our tales involved the Lady of the *Lake*, and why Avalon and Tír na nÓg were often referred to as islands or the Land Beneath the Waves."

The hope unfurling in my chest didn't wither or crumble but grew larger. A shining pearl that started to fill me with soft, gentle light. "I don't need a tree. I need water."

"Maybe." Mordred's eyes flashed brighter, catching the light growing inside me. "But I suspect that you won't have to get wet at all."

"How?"

"If my theory is correct, and Avalon is just another name for the otherworldly plane where the fae live, then a passage to Tír na nÓg will work the same as the Chalice Well."

Bors grunted and shoved away from the wall. "So you're

telling us that we need to find a fucking fairy mound to get to Merlin?"

"Not at all." Laughing, Mordred wheeled his chair back around to his laptop and brought up a browser window. "We need a *burial* mound."

9

BORS

There wasn't much that I hadn't faced in the many centuries of my lives. The original Sir Bors had been the only surviving knight to return from the grail quest. But even I wasn't too keen on wandering around a burial mound. Especially if that meant putting our queen at risk.

"What's the matter, Bors?" Grinning, Mordred glanced back over his shoulder. "Afraid we might run into a few spooky shades?"

I fingered the leather-wrapped pommel of the sword hanging at my hip. "Aye, things that can't die again are more dangerous than things that bleed."

"Agreed," Lance said. "We have enough trouble on our hands without disturbing the dead, let alone the fae. From what I remember of the stories, they don't take too kindly to intruders."

My nerves itched. I tightened my fingers on the pommel, fighting down the urge to draw my sword. We weren't in any danger. So why were my internal alarms sounding?

Worse, my queen noticed my turmoil. She turned her head, studying me with those solemn bottomless eyes.

Drowning me in emotion. Wave after wave of longing, love, and agony flooded me. Centuries of waiting for her to call me. Lifetimes of dying, watching her from afar. Dying in her defense. Dying to reach her. Dying before I even caught sight of her.

Endless yearning. Aching. Desperate to see her. So much pain. So much need.

I couldn't begin to count the number of times I'd been reborn—but I could count the times I'd actually touched Guinevere on one hand.

"I'm here," she whispered, cupping my cheeks in her hands.

But I couldn't see her. Swept away in a tidal wave, I was drowning. I couldn't breathe. Darkness filled me. Brutal cold. I sank deeper and deeper, waiting to reach the bottom, but it never came.

She dug her fingers into my cheeks, a lifeline against the tide sucking me under. "Come back, Bors. I won't let you go. Not this time. Not ever. Bors!"

Drowning. I couldn't hold on. I couldn't find my way back. Too much pain. Too much darkness. A soft voice echoed eerily through the water. *"The lake knows your name."*

Something bright and jagged cut through my mind like a broken sword. A merciless vise gripped my throat. Pain clouded the water, but this was good pain. Wholesome. Clean. It washed away the darkness and the world stopped sinking. My feet struck soft, gleaming sand. The bottom firmed. Grounding me.

I sucked in a deep breath and choked.

Salty water filled my mouth. My shirt was wet.

Panting, I stared down into my queen's stricken eyes. "What the fuck was that?"

My throat ached, my words raw and broken. It took me a moment to realize it was because Lance still had my throat tight in his fist. His left arm locked around my waist, pinning me against him. His right hand squeezed my throat. If we'd been in bed, alone…

That left hand would have been wrapped around my cock while he pounded deep into my ass.

I shuddered, unable to breathe again, but this time because of longing. Goddess, it had been so long. Too long. But we hadn't dared come together very often until our queen called us, even though it'd been almost four hundred years.

He knew exactly how to ground me. How to bring me back when I was drowning. Nothing cut through that darkness like pain, sex, or better yet, both.

Guilt strangled me harder than his fingers. My queen had finally called me. She'd claimed me against all odds. How could I still yearn for her knight's touch, when I had her? It felt so terribly wrong and disrespectful to even…

"Don't be ridiculous." Eyes flashing, she leaned up on her tiptoes and glared at me. "You've always loved Lance. He's always loved you. Why would I ever stand between you? I love you both. I'm not offended in the slightest."

His fingers loosened, making it easier for me to breathe, but he kept his arms around me. With my queen before me, and Lance at my back, the horrible sensation of drowning retreated.

She stroked my cheek, her fingers gentle. As if I might break. "You've had this happen before?"

I shook my head. "Not like this. Not this bad. I have memories of drowning, but I've never been wet before. How is that possible? From a bad dream?"

Lance rested his chin on my shoulder. "I have terrible memories from our past lives."

He didn't elaborate, but we all knew that he still had nightmares of being trapped by Elaine Shalott. Of being raped by her. Repeatedly. Even though he'd never even seen her in this lifetime.

It was such a thing of shame for a man to have been abused by a woman, but especially for a knight and Blood of Sir Lancelot du Lac's caliber. An alpha Blood, who was also the best and most famous knight of the Round Table. He'd endured so much in the lifetimes of this curse. Though I felt the shadowed places in his mind, and the brittle areas that he feared would shatter one day and endanger one of us, I knew his extreme honor. His immortal strength. His endless love.

He had endured unspoken torment at the hands of another queen because his oaths sworn in blood had demanded it. Because once, a thousand years ago and more, he'd fallen in love with our beautiful queen. He still blamed himself for the wretched centuries of this curse. If he'd never fallen in love with Guinevere...

Then I would not be here. Loving him, and loving our queen.

"I would drown a million times to be here with you both now."

Gwen laid her head over my heart. "And I would burn in the tower a million times to love you again. Can you tell me about your nightmare? It could be important."

I wrapped my arms around her and fought the urge to crush her against me. "I suppose it's from my first life as Bors, when my brother, Lionel, and I were taken by the Lady of the Lake as boys."

"Passage through water," she whispered, turning her face up to mine. "But you remember drowning?"

Nodding, I clenched my teeth, fighting to keep control of my emotions. I didn't want to be swept away into the nightmare again.

"I was also supposedly raised by the Lady of the Lake," Lance added. "But I don't remember much. I don't even remember her name or what the house or castle looked like. Do you?"

I shook my head. "She said something to me this time. 'The lake knows your name.' What does that mean? Which lake?"

"I'd hazard to guess that it's not a specific lake at all." Mordred sat before his computers, though he'd turned his chair back to look at us. His face was carefully neutral, but I read a deep pang of loneliness in his bond. He wasn't jealous of our connection to our queen—merely wishing he carried the same level of emotion that bound us to her. If he was tormented by something in his past lives, he'd never said a word. "The Lady of the Lake was probably telling you that if you ever needed passage through the portal to the Otherworld, that your name is the key to open the door."

Our alpha, always present and concerned with any of our needs, loosened his hold on me and stepped closer to Mordred. A hand on his shoulder, focusing his attention on the other man. Giving him the weight of respect and gratitude for all the work and research he'd done to try and help our queen long before she ever called us. "What burial mound were you thinking of?"

"Newgrange." Mordred turned back to his screen, enlarging a picture of the famous Neolithic mound. "It predates the Egyptian pyramids and Stonehenge. Oddly enough, it's also almost completely surrounded by water, making it at least symbolically an island as well."

"You think this is a portal to Avalon?" Gwen asked. "Even though it's in Ireland, right?"

He nodded. "There are numerous mounds like this scattered all through the United Kingdom, but Newgrange is the largest and most famous. It was supposedly the home of the Dagda, a god of the Tuatha dé Danann."

Gwen paced back and forth, her fingers absently playing

with the crescent moon on her necklace. "A god worries me. I've gained my power, and I am stronger than Guinevere has probably been in several lifetimes. But even with Shara's help, I wouldn't want to take on a god. We barely managed to handle Arthur before he could kill us all."

Arthur wouldn't have killed her. The thought of what she would have suffered at his hands made my stomach churn. The wet cotton clung to my chest, chill and damp. An unwelcome reminder of the drowning vision. I pulled the soaked T-shirt over my head. At least my jeans were still dry.

"As long as we're respectful, I don't see why we'd have an issue with the Dagda," Mordred continued. "Supposedly all the Tuatha dé Danann withdrew to Tír na nÓg long ago. If the heart tree can take us somewhere nearby, then we've managed to bypass *her* trap. If it doesn't work, we can try Stonehenge or one of the other stone circles, though that's a little closer to her territory than I'd care to take you."

"What are the risks?" Lance asked. "Are there any queens in the area that we know of?"

"The closest documented nest that's well known is actually in Edinburgh, where the Academy of Blood is located. There are several smaller nests scattered throughout the area, but they're highly localized. Their queens might sense us, but they're not going to be aggressive unless we come near them."

"Unless they're allied with *her* and notify her of our presence," Gwen muttered darkly.

Mordred huffed and gave her a long-suffering look. "My queen, I'm mortally offended that you think I wouldn't have already mapped out her alliances so that we stay far, far away from them."

Softening, she stepped closer to him and draped her arms around his shoulders. "Forgive me, my Blood. Of course you've mapped, color-coded, and documented them for the past thousand years, haven't you?"

"Hardly."

She nipped playfully at his ear. "Are you sure about that?"

Chuckling, he opened a plain manila folder with a flat map of the world. Only two red dots marred the surface. One in England, and the other…

"The only other ally she had for many years was you, my queen."

She closed her eyes, her breath sighing out. "Once she had me under her control, nothing else mattered."

I didn't know what to say. The thought of our queen having to serve Elaine Shalott for hundreds of years made my blood boil in my veins. I couldn't imagine how horrible it'd been for Gwen.

Knowing that we existed. That we fought to stay alive for her.

But if she tried to call us to her…

Elaine waited like a foul spider to pick us off one by one until she managed to snag her true quarry.

"So." That single word shimmered in the air, casting ripples of power through the room, drawing our gazes to our queen's shining eyes. She straightened, and the weight of her presence filled the room. Tendrils of her power seeped into me.

Deep in a primordial forest, a giant stag with massive sweeping antlers raised his regal head. Alert. Ready.

"We have a plan, thanks to Mordred's diligence. At midnight, we'll use the heart tree to travel to Newgrange, and then we'll find out if the legends are true."

"At midnight, my queen?" Lance asked slowly, his manner carefully respectful—but also unsure why we didn't travel immediately to at least see if Mordred's theory was right.

Her gaze settled on me, tracing the complicated patterns

of ink in my chest. Goddess help me. The glancing attention of my queen's gaze was enough to bring me to my knees.

"I want to free Merlin as soon as possible, of course. But a few more hours shouldn't change the outcome, and I'd like to ensure it's dark when we arrive and leave. He's been imprisoned for hundreds of years already. Waiting a few hours gives me time to ensure we're ready."

Now it was Lance's turn to stiffen with an affronted wrinkle across his brow. "We're ready now. We but await your direction."

She glided closer to me. Sweat beaded on my upper lip. My fangs throbbed. I fought to keep them sheathed, not betraying my hunger. I couldn't hide my response in the bond, but I would at least not stand here drooling with my fangs out.

Or perhaps I would. Her index finger traced the words "my queen" inked over my heart.

"*I'm* not ready yet. I must be at full power before this battle."

I dropped to my knees and turned my head to bare my throat. "Take me, my queen. My blood is yours."

She bent down toward me, but only lightly kissed the frantic thumping of my pulse in my neck. "I will, my Blood. But only while my alpha slakes your desire in my bed."

10

LANCE

Goddess help me. My queen's words undid me. They undid Bors. And between the conflagration of desire flooding our bonds...

It was all I could do not to fall at her feet as well.

Yet I hesitated. What she asked... was complicated. Impossibly so.

I didn't say anything, but Bors felt my reluctance in the bond. Stricken, he dropped his chin to his chest. Head bowed. Slumped.

It broke my heart. It broke her heart. She looked at me, her eyes dark with pain and understanding.

There was no question that I loved Bors as much as he loved me. I'd love to fuck him. I had fucked him several times in the centuries we'd roamed the earth, waiting for our queen. It'd been incredible.

Raw. Violent. Rough. The way we both liked it.

When our queen wasn't involved.

And that was the rub. When I was with Bors, I became a different person. One I often regretted later. I didn't mind sharing that side of me with him, but I *did* mind letting our queen see me like that.

Vicious, hard, out of control. I wasn't a caring, protective alpha when I was with him. I was all beast. All dominance. And by goddess, he was going to pay dearly in sweat and pain before I was finished.

I didn't want her to ever fear that I would come to her the same way. Or worse, that I preferred the violent side of myself that I would never share with her. I'd rather slit my throat than make her feel second choice.

"It's not about choice." She wrapped her arms around Bors' head and pulled him against her. "It's about love, and there's no shortage of love in this room."

"Then you misunderstand everything, my queen." She flinched at the harsh edge in my voice, but I couldn't help it. Looking at him, on his knees, broken and hurting and needing...

It stirred the beast inside me. The dark side that I tried so hard to keep buried and chained.

"It's not about love. It's about pain."

She nodded, stroking her fingers over Bors' skull. "You love him enough to give him the pain he needs."

"The violence. The darkness." I clenched my hands into fists, fighting the urge to grab him and sling him across the room.

Into our queen's bed.

"It's not a pretty sight, my queen. You haven't..." My voice cracked on a rumbling growl. "Seen me. Like that."

"I want to see all of you. I love you, Lance. As much as I love him. As much as you love him. I'm not afraid."

But I am. I didn't say it aloud, but I didn't have to. She heard.

She reached up and pulled a pin out of her hair, letting the strands fall free. She didn't wear her hair as long as Guinevere of old, but it took her a few minutes to unravel the braid to free her lustrous hair.

Something the famous knight would never have been privileged to witness.

His lady queen, letting down her hair. For bed.

When her lord husband, the king, awaited her.

"Mordred," she called softly. "Would you carry me to bed?"

He leaped to his feet and swept her up into his arms. "At once, my queen."

Striding into the adjacent room, he set her gently on the edge of her bed. Wordlessly, she lifted her arms over her head, inviting him to pull the sweater off. She lifted each foot, and he diligently untied her shoes and set them aside. Her jeans took more work.

Luscious work that had me sweating, unable to look away.

Bors fared even worse. Eyes wide and dark, he shot a pleading glance at me. *:Help me. Before I do something foolish. Like throw myself at her feet and sob with relief that she's still alive.:*

Without answering, I slowly unsheathed my sword, letting steel sing in the silence. Relief washed away the tenseness in his face. This, we knew. Warfare. Sword in hand. The clang of steel. We'd sparred against each other in every lifetime, and he knew he could never beat me.

No one would best me with a sword. So it had been from the very beginning.

Though this wasn't about him trying to beat me, or displaying our skills for our queen, though she would undoubtedly enjoy the show. Over the lifetimes of our curse, we'd taken swordplay to an entirely new level.

It was one thing to meet another skilled warrior in hand-to-hand combat with the intent of causing bodily injury or death. It was quite another level to defeat him with razor-sharp steel—without drawing a single drop of blood.

Without our queen, the closest we could ever get to the warriors we'd once been was with swords in hand. Centuries fell away. The modern world crumbled into dust. I had never served as a knight or ridden into battle on horseback, but when I held a sword, I was Lancelot du Lac.

And no one could defeat me.

Rolling my head side to side and loosening my shoulders, I stepped into the open space in the center of her bedchamber. Bors paused long enough to shuck his boots and pants. If we couldn't wear full chainmail and armor as knights of old, we typically fought naked. It certainly made what came after easier if we were already nude, and neither of us cared to pause in the middle of our spar to remove our clothes so we could fuck.

I laid my sword down on the foot of her bed to free my hands. "You don't want to challenge me into slicing off those jeans inch by inch this time?"

Bors grinned as I unbuttoned my pants and toed off my boots. "Fuck, no. I like these jeans. I would have killed to have a pair as comfortable back in the day. Leather chafes like a mofo."

I pulled the T-shirt over my head and grunted in agreement. "This modern world does have some conveniences."

"Did Guinevere ever watch you fight each other like this?" Gwen's sultry voice drew my attention to her. Mordred sat in the middle of her bed, leaning back against the headboard, with our queen braced between his thighs so she could see the show.

Not that he cared in the slightest about watching us spar, when our queen's perfect body beckoned. He cupped her breasts in each hand, his fingers lazily rolling her nipples. Nuzzling her throat, licking behind her ear, gently teasing with his fangs. I could feel the buzz of pleasure in her bond. Her rising desire as he diligently stoked the flames in her body.

The scent of her need drove foot-long spikes in my skull. Goddess help me when I smelled her blood.

"Naked as a jaybird?" Bors drawled. "Never. Arthur would have been apoplectic at the thought."

I bared my teeth at him and let out a rumbling growl. "Don't say his fucking name."

Standing loose and casual in the center of the room, Bors almost managed to look bored. "Arthur fucking Pendragon? That name?"

Hairline cracks splintered across my control. I gritted my teeth, fighting to beat down the beast before it could slip free. Even though that was exactly what Bors wanted most of all. "I'll wipe that fucking name off your mouth with my fist."

"Be my guest."

My blood pumped. Mighty wings unfurled. Poisoned tail arched inside me, vicious tip ready to attack. Claws unsheathed.

The manticore bellowed a challenge, eager for battle.

So much of my legendary image was a complete sham. Lancelot, the famed knight, honorable and chivalrous to a fault. The cool, collected warrior who rode the countryside doing good deeds. A shining example of the Round Table.

All lies. All fairy tales as wild and far-fetched as King Arthur being the lauded king who united Briton with goodness and law.

This was me. The real me.

The cracks widened. Teeth bared, I seized my sword and charged my best friend and closest companion as if I was going to behead him.

GWEN

I n the centuries since I'd matured as a queen, though forbidden to call my Blood, I'd fantasized about my knights. I'd imagined them donning armor and swords to fight once again, even if only for my amusement. But in all those delicious daydreams in nearly four hundred years, I'd never been able to conjure anything quite like this.

My two knights. Naked. Aroused. Sweating. Furiously beating each other in a flurry of swords and fists that I could barely follow.

Light and fast on his feet, Lance blurred every time he moved. I couldn't even keep my eyes on him. It was easier to watch the way Bors reacted. His head snapping back after Lance's fist collided with his mouth as promised. His sword flashing as he tried to deflect Lance's blows. I flinched at the clash and screech of metal on metal, braced for blood.

My power rose inside me, stirred both by my arousal— and my fear that I might need to heal one of them before this was over.

But to my shock, no cuts appeared on Bors' chest, even when I knew that Lance had struck him. I couldn't follow the sword as it rose and fell, but Bors staggered back and doubled over, his breath wheezing. So the blow had landed.

Mordred's breath was hot in my ear. "They didn't dare bleed for fear another Aima would smell them and recognize who they were."

"They didn't feed?" My voice trembled, my breath catching on a soft sigh as his fingers glided down my stomach. "At all?"

"They learned to feed in other ways." He gripped my earlobe in his teeth, letting the tips of his fangs prick my skin without drawing blood. "Sex. Violence. They feed on it as surely as they'll cease trading blows as soon as they catch the scent of your blood. Shall I prove it for you, my queen?"

I opened my thighs wider, arching up against his hand. "Yes."

"Watch them," he whispered, licking my ear. "See how quickly they come to you."

He stroked deeper, drawing another groan from my lips. My pussy tightened, aching with need. My fangs pulsed, sending tiny shockwaves through my core. It would be so easy to come. Just the slightest brush of his fingers...

Shuddering, I bit my lip as climax rippled through me. I tasted my blood. My power spilled down my spine and limbs, making me tremble and glow with a soft white nimbus.

The vicious crashes ceased. My breathing was loud in the silence. Blinking, I managed to open my eyes and focus on Bors. Staring at me, he stood hunched slightly, as if his ribs pained him. His bottom lip was swollen. One eye blackened.

He licked his lips, tossed the sword aside, and leaped for the bed.

Lance slammed him down onto the floor with a crash that made me cry out.

"Now we've done it." Mordred chuckled, rubbing his mouth back and forth against my ear and the delicate hollow behind my jaw. "You thought they fought before, but now, the true challenge begins. Will Bors be able to get his mouth on you before Lance gets inside him?"

They rolled and thumped. Thrashing elbows and grunts of pain. Solid thuds against flesh. They disappeared from my line of vision, but something rocked the bed hard enough wood cracked. Hopefully the entire frame didn't collapse on them.

Scrambling up the side of the mattress, Bors dug his fingers into the bedding, only to lose his grip and fall back down onto the floor. By the crash, it sounded like he'd cracked his skull open on the floor.

In the bond, I felt fireworks exploding in *both* of their heads. So he must have head-butted Lance rather than the floor. He exploded up again and managed to grab my ankle. My knee. I started to slide across the mattress, but Mordred tightened his hold on me, providing an anchor for Bors to haul himself up onto the bed with us.

Lance came flying up from the floor like a pouncing lion. Eyes blazing, his mouth open on a roar of fury, fingers partially shifted into claws. He raked bloody grooves down Bors' back, but he refused to let go of me.

Jamming his clawed fist into Bors' side, my alpha seized Bors' shoulder in his jaws and shook him like a rag doll. But that didn't stop Bors from wriggling closer so he could seal his mouth over my clit.

"Point for Bors." Mordred's cheer turned to a choking wheeze when Lance reached over me and grabbed his throat, hauling him nose to nose with him.

"Why the fuck aren't you inside her already?"

I arched up against Bors, grinding against his mouth. "Yes, please."

The words were barely out of my mouth, and Mordred lifted me enough to push inside me. Surprised, since I didn't remember him taking his clothes off, I gasped and bucked up against Bors. He wrapped his arms around my thighs, pinning me between them. Pushing deeper, Mordred didn't even have to thrust. Not with Bors sucking on my clit.

Tension coiled inside me. Twisting and writhing between my powerful knights, I watched Lance pull back. Eyes blazing, he sat back on his heels, lazily stroking himself.

His gaze traced the powerful lines of my knight's back. The rounded muscles of his ass. The explosive power in his thick thighs. Then he met my gaze and let me see the raw emotion shredding his heart.

He enjoyed looking at my other Blood, though it wasn't something he indulged in often. Concealing his reactions, especially his desire, both for me and for Bors, was so ingrained in him that even centuries later, he hesitated in making himself vulnerable.

Even to me.

This time, he didn't try to hide his arousal. His dick swelled in his fist. His neck and shoulders corded with effort as he restrained himself.

"You're in luck, Bors." He smeared his fingers in the blood dripping down Bors' back and smeared the blood down his crack to act as lube. "I won't tear you a new asshole this time."

11

BORS

He thought he was such a terrible person for doing this to me. So what did that make me?

Because I fucking loved it when I was bloody and bruised for him. We were Aima warriors, so I could take a hell of a lot of damage. Even better, he could actually hurt me enough to make me bleed now that we were with our queen. We didn't have to worry one of Elaine's goons might sniff us out.

Though I couldn't resist lifting my head from Gwen's pussy a moment—just to make sure she really didn't mind this. Her bond bathed me in scorching flames, but maybe that was just Mordred's dick filling her up. I'd once been pretty fucking talented with my tongue, but I was extremely out of practice after generations of never even reaching her side before I was cut down by our enemies.

As soon as I lifted my head, she ran her fingers over my skull. My face. Her other arm was thrown back over her shoulder so she could clutch Mordred's neck. Eyes wide and dark, she stared at Lance, her lips softly parted. Her tongue flicked out to tease the tips of her fangs and stroke the full curve of her bottom lip. I didn't think she was aware that she did it. It wasn't a deliberate ploy to drive me crazy.

Though that was certainly the result.

I started to move up her body so she could sink those glorious fangs into my throat.

Lance's forearm locked around my neck and he hauled me up on my knees against him. "Oh no you don't," he growled roughly against my ear. "Let her see what kind of animals we are."

He had the claws. All I had were antlers and hooves, neither of which were useful to attack an enemy from the rear. The best I could do was to pound his face a few times, increasingly frantic as he tightened the headlock and throttled me.

As I lost the ability to breathe…

I lost myself.

Maybe it was only the childhood trauma creeping back in to fuck with my head, but I'd come to accept it over the centuries. I'd even decided that I'd drowned that first time as a child—because this was what I needed most of all.

I *needed* to drown.

I needed to sink beneath the waters and into cold, empty darkness. Nothing mattered here except the urge to fight and drive toward the light. If I managed to break free and swim to the light, then I would live again. I had to fight to live. I had to fight to breathe.

That fight reminded me every single day why I was still here. Why I kept returning lifetime after lifetime, always searching. Always drowning.

Lance had always been the light for me. The most gallant knight. Round Table hero. Queen's champion. I couldn't remember the years we must have spent together growing up with the Lady of the Lake, but it was his face I searched for as soon as I remembered what and who I was.

Not my brother's. Never my king's.

I'd always known that if I could get to Lance, I might live to see our queen again. He was my only hope. Without him...

I would die before I could ever drown in our queen's love again.

I thrashed against him. I choked. I wheezed. I dug ineffective nails into his flesh and tried to gouge out his eyes. I would have howled and screamed if I could get any air into my lungs.

He waited until I was frothing at the mouth like a rabid wolf, completely consumed with my fight to breathe. Then he shoved his dick into me, skewering me until he was balls deep. Only then did he loosen his grip on my throat enough to let me gulp for air.

Though he immediately tightened his arm again. Darkness hovered, black spots swelling and dancing in my vision. I couldn't do anything but hang in his grasp and wait desperately for him to decide when I would breathe again. A quick gulp. A choking gasp. Then darkness. Again. While he drove into me mercilessly.

He was the dark water taking me under. The sweet promise of death and peace in the end. It was a lie. We both knew it. Guinevere's knights would never have peace until we broke Arthur's curse. Even if it took another thousand years.

The curse would go on and on like this endless ocean of pain and darkness and misery. Until Lance let another crack of hope pour into my lungs. Until a speck of light filtered down through millions of miles of agony to show me the way back to the surface.

Back to our queen.

The blackness faded enough that I could see her face. She glided down through the waters, floating closer. Shining like a captured star. Soft, pearly white flowed around her in the water. Clothes, maybe. Her power. I wasn't sure. But it looked like wings. Flowing gossamer wings of dreams and love and hope. So perfect. So beautiful.

I wanted to say something. I wanted to tell her that I loved her. More than anything. More than my life. More, even, than Lance's life. Because if we lost her...

I would lose him. Again.

And I didn't know how many more times I could endure such loss without giving up and letting the cold darkness claim me at last.

Her lips pressed to mine. Searing hot against the cold. Bright against the dark. She breathed for me. She hoped. She loved. For me.

She *bled* for me. I could see the red spreading in the water. I breathed her in. Letting the taste of her fill me. Crystal moonlight. White lilies. Seductive and graceful, seemingly delicate and fragile. Though I had enough wits about me to know that was a lie too.

Nothing fragile would have survived all these centuries just to hold us again, even if only for a short while.

A crushing weight drove me down, deeper into darkness. I went willingly, letting Lance carry me down. Because our queen floated with me. Her hands on my face. Her blood on my tongue. Her love shining inside me.

Forever.

GWEN

I fought back tears, because I didn't want to upset either of them. My tears carried regret and sadness and pain.

But only because we had lost so much. They'd endured so much. For so long.

Bors lay unconscious in my arms. Lance had fucked him savagely until they'd both collapsed against me. He wasn't able to lift his head yet, or even roll to the side to give me room to breathe. Not that I minded in the slightest.

I'd known they must be suffering out in the world. Fully aware that I lived—but for some unknown reason, unable to call them to my side. That uncertainty had been their torture. Afraid that any moment I would be captured or killed by Arthur before they ever even saw me in this life.

Of course, my torture was the same. Afraid Arthur would kill them before I was free of Elaine's geas. Afraid she might find Lance first. I hadn't really feared for myself, but I also hadn't understood the deep, personal suffering they each endured all these lifetimes. Especially Bors.

I'd never known that he'd drowned as a child. Had the original Guinevere known? Somehow… I didn't think so. She'd never been allowed to get this close to Bors. To know his heart and fears. The only person he'd ever had in his life to rely on was Lance. At least he'd been able to take care of him all these years, even if they'd feared to indulge very often.

Turning enough to see Mordred's face, I asked him, "Do you have something like this that torments you?"

His dick was still inside me, though I'd felt him come along with Lance and Bors. We'd all climaxed like dominoes, unable to hold back the overwhelming emotion pouring from them both.

"Nothing so dramatic as drowning," he said lightly, though I felt an echo in his bond of soul-deep pain.

I wriggled out from beneath my Bloods' dead weights so I could more fully face him. "Tell me. Please."

"I'm destined to die alone." A wry smile twisted his lips. "That's all."

But it wasn't all. I felt a heavy sense of overwhelming failure in his bond. *Personal* failure. As if he blamed himself for every horrible thing that Arthur had ever done. "You were never the one who was supposed to kill him and free us."

He shrugged slightly. "If we ever live long enough to see Camlann again, then we shall see who walks away."

"You haven't faced him on the battlefield since the first time?"

"Never. I'm always dead before then. It's a relief, honestly. I'd rather die first than see what he does to you."

"The first battle...do you remember what happened?"

He closed his eyes a moment, as if he was pulling up the memory to look at it from all angles. "His heart," he finally ground out. "I'm trying to pierce his heart. No. Actually, I'm trying to tear it out." Opening his eyes, he laughed and shook his head. "Fat lot of good an eagle's talons did against dragon hide."

His golden eyes were shadowed, burnished and aged like an antique coin buried for centuries. I tried to bring some of the spark back to his eyes. "Let's try to rip his heart out when he's a man, then."

He snorted. "Easier said than done. He knows he's vulnerable as a man. It's the same reason he always managed to have Lancelot sent away from court when he committed his most outrageous sins against you, my queen. He couldn't risk Lancelot formally challenging him before witnesses."

"Because he knew Lance would win," I said slowly, nodding.

Groaning, Lance lifted his head and blinked at me

blearily. "Nobody has ever defeated Lancelot du Lac with a sword, but he's arrogant enough after so many generations of this curse that he probably thinks he can."

I didn't realize Bors was awake until I felt the chiding sting of his teeth on my shoulder, though he didn't break the skin. "You were supposed to feed on me, my queen. We need you strong."

I nuzzled against Mordred's neck, reached back and found Lance's arm to tug around me like a blanket, and wriggled my ass back against Bors' groin. His dick stirred. Again. Making me smile. "I did."

"Bullshit," he retorted, snapping his teeth playfully against my ear.

I closed my eyes and drank them in. My three Blood. Alive. Together at last. All I wanted to do was touch them. Hold them. Love them. As long as possible. Before...

I swallowed hard and curled Lance's arm tighter to my chest.

This time... I would hold them. Forever.

12

GWEN

The ghastly white branches of Shara's heart tree gleamed in the soft glow from my necklace. In the complete darkness of Isador Tower's basement, the soft, pearly light from my crescent moon was welcome. I suspected I would need even more light before this journey was complete, so I didn't try to tamp down my light.

Let this be a warning to Arthur or whoever we encounter. Camelot shines again.

I took several deep breaths to center myself and set my mind on where I wanted to go. Newgrange, the massive round stone tomb. I pictured the gleaming stones shining in the moonlight. Mordred had shown me pictures of the entrance, blocked by a heavy stone carved in spirals.

Symbols of the Great Mother. Three spirals.

Triune. Triskeles. Triple Goddess.

The same ancient symbols replicated through dozens of civilizations. We were all united. All descended from Her. Mother Earth, Gaia, Danu, Dea Matrona. So many other names across all the cultures of the world.

Aima or Tuatha dé Danann. Vampire or fairy queen. We were descended from Her daughters.

At last, it was time for this vampire queen to pierce the veil and retrieve my wizard.

I didn't open my eyes as I stepped into the dark hole within the tree's trunk. I trusted it would take me where I needed to go. Lance held my right hand, Mordred my left. Bors walked at my back, gripping each of my other Blood's shoulders. Soon I would have Merlin before me. I would be surrounded by my Blood.

Four corners. Four points. I needed that fourth point before I encountered Arthur again. I had to be complete.

Power hummed all around me, amplifying with each step. I wasn't deliberately calling my power, but I felt the dance and spark inside me. I didn't try to suppress it. For all I knew, I'd need every drop available at my fingertips to survive.

Vibrations rumbled my bones, making my fangs throb with my heartbeat. No blood, not yet, but it would only take a second and I'd tear my lips open and release the full weight of my power.

I felt an opening ahead, a sense of widening that made me open my eyes.

Covered in ancient symbols, a flat stone lay before us. A dark doorway lay beyond in a stone wall that rose to a gently domed roof. The waning moon hung low in the sky in a sprinkling of stars. Something red blazed across the sky, a brilliant flaming meteor gone in seconds. But it seemed momentous. The air weighed heavily, and the vibrations deepened, a throb that hurt my ears even though there wasn't any sound. Magic pulsed in the heavy air, lifting the delicate hairs on my nape.

I paused and looked back over my shoulder. We hadn't exited a tree, or anything, really. But a pair of standing stones marked the front entrance on either side of us.

"Imagine this place thousands of years ago," Mordred whispered reverently. "How much magic would have been held here when all the standing stones lined the boundary. It would have eclipsed the power at Stonehenge."

Still holding my Bloods' hands, I stepped closer to the mound's entrance. A flat lintel stone covered the low doorway. The waiting passageway was too narrow for us all to walk side by side.

Bors brushed past us, taking the lead down the dark hallway. My light still shone, illuminating the carved stones. Above, an immense weight of earth and stone pressed downward. Entombing us. The walls closed in, the channel narrowing. The smell of ancient earth and old, old blood tantalized my tongue. Not human blood. Not animal.

This smelled like... Her, the Mother of all things. The pulsing magic around us was Her heartbeat. This tunnel, Her birth canal, from which all life had flowed. That was how old and powerful this site felt.

My light gleamed brighter as we went deeper. I shone like the full moon on pure white sands or pristine snow. This place called to the White Enchantress, welcoming me home with open arms.

:Was Guinevere ever here?: I asked my Blood. *:This place feels familiar.:*

:No tale places her here that I'm aware of,: Mordred replied. *:But it's possible. It's certainly not far from Glastonbury Tor and Stonehenge. If she was as powerful as we think, then it'd be likely that she would have visited and even used all of these ancient sites.:*

I halted before a low stone altar. Images flickered through my mind, whether imagination or fragile memories from past lives, I wasn't sure. Torches flickered on either end of the altar. A woven white cloth covered the stone. Flowers and freshly baked bread. Flasks of wine or mead. Offerings to the Goddess.

I was suddenly glad I'd worn white. The simple cotton gown looked more like a vintage nightgown than anything a modern woman would wear, but it'd felt right. Even if it would show dirt or blood.

That was the point, after all.

I punctured my bottom lip deeply enough to allow blood to dribble freely down my chin, splattering my bodice. "Great Mother, we honor You. I seek my Blood, Merlin, whom I believe is held in the Otherworld beyond the veil. Please grant us passage to the Land Beneath the Waves so that I might hold my beloved once more."

I suddenly smelled the salty sea, even though we were surely too far from the coast to smell the ocean. I turned to my right, letting the salty air guide me. Lance went ahead of me, leading the way. Bors hesitated, and I felt a surge of terror in the bond. He'd drowned before. He didn't care to drown again.

"Stay here and wait for us."

He shook his head, his mouth hardening to a grim slant. "Never, my queen. I said I'd drown a million times to be with you, and I meant it."

I held my hand out to him and he seized my fingers in a death grip. Lance took my other hand, and I paused a moment, waiting for Mordred to take Bors' hand, or at least touch him so we were all connected. My necklace's glow rippled in the air ahead of us. Tiny sparkles and diamonds reflected the light back to us in a complicated design. Almost as though a spider had woven her web across the tunnel, though it seemed to be more of a transparent curtain. The threads wove toward the center in a circular spiral that caught my light in glistening dewdrops, brightening as we neared.

"The veil," Mordred whispered hoarsely. "I didn't know we'd actually be able to see it."

Lance ran his hand over the surface, and it waved and rippled like an airy tapestry made of nothing but gossamer web. "At least we won't get wet. Ready, my queen?"

I closed my eyes and focused on my will. From Guinevere's memories, I pictured Merlin in my mind. Shoulder-length hair, shining silver with a delicate lavender tint he'd always sworn to be natural. Large midnight blue eyes, slightly tilted and deep set, giving him an elven look, emphasized by his high, chiseled cheekbones. He'd once sworn to never bow to anyone. King, queen, dragon, demon—it didn't matter. He had his own power. He didn't need anything or anyone.

He feared nothing.

Until he fell in love with Queen Guinevere, and then lost her.

As a girl, I'd stood on the edge of the Chalice Well and felt his presence on the other side. He was that commanding. That powerful and compelling. Humans whispered that he'd been conceived by a demon on a human woman, and even Aima houses feared him. He wasn't a king, but he possessed an impressive gift that had made him famous as a wizard even in this day and age.

I sensed him beyond the thin, shining curtain. A massive magnet drawing my focus. Darkness to my light.

Squeezing my Bloods' hands, I stepped through the veil. "Merlin, I'm coming!"

13

GWEN

My skin tingled as we stepped through the shimmering veil. Rainbows exploded all around us, blinding me. Still blinking to clear my vision, it took me a moment to realize we were through.

Dazzling colors surrounded us. Cotton-candy pink and sky blue, orchid purple and acid green, flaming orange and neon yellow. Trees and flowers of impossible color combinations, growing in a wild, lush tumble everywhere. Tinkling sparks hung in air that was thick and heavy with the scent of flowers. Living walls of ivy and tumbling flowers blew in the gentle breeze, giving me a glimpse of a fountain, only instead of water, an oil-slick rainbow fluid splashed on the shining stone.

A low drone filled my ears, as if a thousand lazy bumblebees danced among the flowers. Birds trilled somewhere in the trees, but it sounded like words instead of tweets and calls. I couldn't understand the language, but I was sure they were words. Almost as if they were singeing a poem or telling a story.

A story about me. Or rather, Guinevere's sad story.

"Do you know who the fairy queen is?" I turned my head toward Mordred...

But he wasn't there. Releasing both my Blood's hands, I turned in a complete circle. His bond was still in my head but stretched so thinly that it was muted. "We have to go back for him."

The shimmering veil we'd crossed through was gone. Gently rolling hills carpeted in lavender and pink stretched into the distance. Water sparkled on the horizon, a sea or lake, I wasn't sure.

"I don't think we can go back." Lance tucked my hand around his arm. "Find Merlin, and then we'll return to find out why Mordred didn't come. But I must admit it's probably a good idea that one Blood stayed behind to protect our flank, even if it wasn't deliberate."

"He wasn't ever associated with the Lady of the Lake," Bors replied. "I bet that's why he couldn't pass through."

They were right, but I still didn't like it. "Neither was I."

The sooner I found Merlin, the sooner we could go back. Hopefully he'd know how to find the appropriate passageway through the veil.

"Without us drowning," Bors muttered.

"You're a queen." A male voice rolled through the dense foliage, impatient and terse, as if he'd already lectured about this topic half a dozen times. "Descended from Guinevere herself, who made a willing sacrifice of your blood in one of the most holy places in Eiru. Of course, the ways opened for you."

Or perhaps that annoyance in his voice was because he'd been imprisoned for hundreds of years, waiting for the chance to lecture me once again. "Merlin? Is that you?"

A curtain of delicate petals lifted, revealing a sparkling white archway and a winding pebbled path. Bors immediately took the lead. Lance stayed beside me, but I could feel his attention sweeping around us, particularly checking over his shoulder to make sure we weren't attacked from behind.

My stomach fluttered with nerves. When I'd seen Lance, I'd recognized him immediately. Even if I'd only heard his voice, I would have known him. My heart would have sung with joy.

If that voice was Merlin... Why didn't he come greet me? Was he trapped or restrained in some way beyond this magical location? Was he angry with me? But for what reason could he possibly be angry with me, when I'd come to release him?

We rounded a tall fluttering bush of softest blues that exploded up into butterflies as we neared. I jumped against Lance, and even Bors' started to unsheathe his sword.

"So twitchy," the man said, this time with a hint of amusement in his voice. "You weren't always so fearful, Sir Bors de Ganis."

Bors slammed the sword back down into its sheath. "Forgive me for not wanting to die again this day when our queen has finally managed to call me to her side once more."

A white rectangular table sat beneath a weeping willow, only its leaves were bright red. My attention immediately locked on the man seated opposite us, positioned to watch us approach the table.

Merlin. He looked exactly the same as if he'd walked out of Guinevere's memories. The sands of time had left him completely unchanged.

He hadn't lived and died countless times as my Blood and I had suffered these past centuries. He hadn't seen us killed by Arthur or Elaine or both. He hadn't seen Lance defeated and imprisoned.

Over and over and over.

His eyes flashed with emotion, darker than the midnight blue that Guinevere remembered. I didn't need a bond with

him to read his rage. His lips were tight, his eyes narrowed
and dark, and he certainly didn't run to greet me.

Lance's bond made a sound like a ringing sword as it
was drawn for battle. *:He doesn't even rise for you, my queen.
Given our very long history and your lineage, that's unforgivably
rude.:*

A woman stood and glided toward us. Gossamer robes
fluttered around her, very much like the butterflies that had
startled us so much. Her skin gleamed a burnished golden-
copper. Darker copper hair hung in a thick braid that trailed
the ground behind her.

"Welcome to Avalon, sister." She kissed both of my cheeks
and took my hand in hers. "I'm so pleased to see you at last."

"Humph." Merlin glared at me. "You might as well have
gallivanted around for another five hundred years. Evidently
I'm in no rush to return to the land of the living."

"I'm sorry, who are you?" I asked her as politely as
possible.

The woman laughed, a high sweet sound like chiming
bells. "My apologies, Guinevere. I forget how much time has
passed for you. My name is Morgan. You once knew me very
well."

"I'm Gwenhwyfar Findabair, though most people call me
Gwen."

She leaned closer, staring into my eyes. A small sound
escaped her lips and her jeweled eyes shimmered. It took me
a second to realize she was near tears. "You honestly don't
remember."

Bewildered, I glanced at Merlin, dressed in deep purple
robes that made his hair gleam like amethysts. "Remember
what? I recognize Merlin, though I have no idea why he's so
angry."

His mouth opened and then snapped shut. His eyes
blazed. His cheeks darkened and he stood jerkily, moving

stiffly as if he was a puppet or robot. "How *dare* you forget that you locked me here for over a thousand years?"

MERLIN

M y rage was a living beast that snarled and tore hunks from my flesh, devouring me slowly for centuries. Even here in the Land Beneath the Waves I felt the excruciating passage of time grain by grain.

So many years. Wasted.

Lifetimes. Destroyed.

Entire civilizations rose and fell.

While I sat here in a beautiful paradise, tormented by my most excellent and vivid imagination of all the horrid things the bastard king would do to my beloved queen. I cursed the day I ever involved myself with House Pendragon.

Even though that relationship had led me straight to Guinevere.

Perhaps my memory had dulled over the years, but this woman looked nothing like the legendary queen. Surely the White Enchantress's blood must run very thinly now. She looked at me, eyes flaring wide with shock, and I didn't recognize her.

Disappointment welled inside me, choking me, but at least it quelled my fury.

"I... I mean, *she* imprisoned you?" Gwen asked. "How is that possible?"

Morgan slipped an arm around her waist and led her closer, seating her on my left. Her knights glared with murderous fury at me, but I ignored them. Their ridiculous oaths of chivalry had always been a hindrance, which was exactly why Lancelot kept falling into Elaine's clutches.

And yes, that was only one of the many reasons that Arthur kept killing them. You couldn't be honorable when battling a poisonous serpent that wanted so very desperately to kill us all. They couldn't help who they were, any more than I could forget what I was. No matter how long I'd had to dwell on all my failures, I couldn't change the past.

Only Guinevere had been able to weave our imperfect pieces together into a tapestry that had shone so brightly that our legend still lived centuries later. Though only a fraction of the truth remained.

"Where to begin?" Morgan sat on my right. The ever-perfect hostess, she poured tea into delicate china that looked like water lilies. "Guinevere was known primarily as a healer to the common folk, but few knew that her greatest gift was foresight."

I couldn't help but make another disgruntled sound. "Too bad she didn't foresee what a mistake marrying Arthur would be."

"Perhaps she did." Morgan gave me a quelling look and continued her tale. "She took as many precautions as possible, else you would not be here, Merlinus. History has lost a great deal of the truth. While she claimed direct lineage to Dea Matrona, her father was Gwyn, the king of the Tylwyth Teg."

She paused, waiting to see if Gwen recognized the name.

Of course, she did not. This inferior imposter knew nothing at all. "The Welsh fairies," I growled. "Guinevere's father was a fairy king."

"Daughter of a goddess and a fairy king." Gwen sipped her tea with a bemused smile curving her lips. "Is that why I was able to pass through the veil?"

Morgan lifted one shoulder in an elegant shrug. "Yes and

no. As an Aima queen, your blood offering would have revealed the veil too. All daughters of the goddesses are welcome here. But you especially are always welcome whether you offer a sacrifice or not. The fae blood still sings in you, though you hear it not."

Her head tipped slightly, as if she listened to the wind and the rustling branches. I held my breath, hoping she might feel the singing in her blood. That she might remember all that we'd lost. But she shrugged and took another sip of her tea.

My shoulders slumped. We had lost so much. So very much. How could we strike down Arthur now after so long? While we'd lost power, he had surely gained in strength, feeding on our misery and all the pain he'd caused.

"Gwyn fancied himself a psychopomp," Morgan continued. "He gathered the souls of the great warriors and brought them to the underworld. Eventually the Tylwyth Teg became associated more with demons than fairies, taking on a darker edge. Gwyn reveled in his power and even kidnapped his sister, and later his nephew. He tortured and murdered at will, spreading the darkness in his realm. It was only years later, after King Arthur visited Annwyn to retrieve the stolen child, that Guinevere learned the truth. Her father had been corrupted by his ring, the gatherer of souls. The more souls it held, the darker and more malevolent its power. When King Arthur returned to your world, he stole Gwyn's ring."

Gwen gasped. "Shara told me that ring was the source of Arthur's power. But Findabair chronicles recorded the ring as Guinevere's wedding gift to him."

"That was the story he put out." My lips twisted sourly. "He loved being able to claim his wife was both queen and fairy, and the ring took on more significance if he claimed his royal father-in-law had gifted the treasure to him as a wedding gift."

"Lying black-hearted bloody bastard," Bors muttered. "Fuck."

I grinned at him. Now I remembered why he'd been one of my favorite knights.

"Freed of the darkness, Gwyn refused to reclaim the ring and charged his daughter with finding a way to destroy it." Morgan sighed, shaking her head. "She saw the darkness spreading through Camelot, twisting Arthur more and more every day. She loved him once and believed that if she could divest him of the ring that he would be the man she loved once more. Everything she did from that moment on was to try and undo the darkness of that cursed ring, for only something fae could destroy it."

"Excalibur was never Arthur's sword," Lance said slowly, his mouth hanging open a moment in shock as the memory emerged.

Morgan nodded. "Excalibur was forged here with the sole purpose of destroying the ring. Nimue placed it in the stone for Guinevere to retrieve, but with the ring's power, Arthur was able to discover their plan and claimed the sword as his own. The story was embellished over the centuries, only adding to his fame and glory."

Gwen focused on me. I searched her face, trying to find any trace of my queen. Maybe her eyes? Though Guinevere's eyes had been brilliant emerald green. This woman's eyes were more muted. Everything about her was grayed. Lesser. Worn down by the passage of centuries. I rubbed my chest absently, trying to ease the ache.

"How and why did Guinevere send you here?"

"We needed another fae-forged weapon. Something small and inconsequential that Arthur wouldn't suspect. After he intercepted the sword, she wanted one of us to come personally and fetch it for her. So she told me, at least. By then, Arthur kept her under careful scrutiny. He would have been suspicious if she opened the veil to send anyone through herself. She refused to ask Bors to drown again, and Lancelot couldn't leave for obvious reasons. I was the only one left who carried fae blood who could go through the veil without her assistance. All very reasonable, yes?"

I growled and slammed my fist down on the table, rattling the teacups. Unable to continue the story. Unable to admit how she'd lied to me. Tricked me. My very own beloved queen.

Morgan rang a crystal bell. Immediately, beautiful young lads dressed in jeweled robes came to clear the spilled tea and broken dishes away. "Guinevere saw the curse unfolding as Arthur's power grew. She saw what would happen to the world if he gained Merlin's power as well as her own. In an attempt to stall the worst of the curse, she sent Merlin to us to protect him. To prevent him from returning, she sacrificed the last of her fae power to lock the passage back until someone of her blood was able to unlock the veil once more."

I pushed up from the chair and paced back and forth alongside the table. "I didn't need protection! I could have blasted him from the sky, torn off his wings and used his black heart in my darkest magicks yet."

"The cost to your soul—" Morgan began.

I cut her off, whirling so hard and fast my robes fluttered about me like wings. "Fuck my soul! I would rather have damned myself for all time than allow my queen to suffer one moment of pain and misery. Instead, the fucking bastard king burned her. Burned her! My queen! Tortured and trapped, doomed to fail generation after generation until all that's left is this… this…" I waved my hand at Gwen. "*Shell* of the great queen we loved. A fraction, a bare shadow, of Guinevere remains, our only hope of defeating him."

"How dare you?" Lance retorted, drawing his sword partway free.

Gwen laid her hand on his arm, stalling his attack. "He's right, Lance."

Breathing hard, he glared at me, the muscles in his arm quivering as he fought to contain his rage and obey. "Never, my queen. You're no shell. Camelot shines once more, and if he's too arrogant to see that…"

I guffawed, even though I'd rather sob at all we'd lost. "You ignorant louts wouldn't have any idea how brightly Camelot once shone. You can't remember how great our queen's nest was, or you'd never even suggest such a thing. I'm sorry, Gwen. I truly don't mean to insult you, but we must face the facts. The truth is that you're nowhere near Guinevere's power, which affects how we proceed."

She stood, her gaze steady, her chin up proudly despite my words. "I may not be as strong as Guinevere, but let me remind you that your great and powerful queen lost to Arthur, not once but countless times over the centuries. She died over and over, heartbroken and alone. Her magic, broken. Her house, destroyed. All that's left of Camelot is standing right here before you."

Tossing her head slightly so her hair fell back from her face, she straightened to her full height. Her body was taller and thicker than my Guinevere, who'd been willowy and delicate thanks to her fae heritage. I'd often joked that she might blow away like dandelion fluff if we didn't hold her down and keep her grounded.

"Guinevere's line hasn't successfully called Blood in generations. I have *three*." A small smile softened her lips, but her eyes flashed with pride and a touch of anger. She rightfully did not count me as Blood. Not yet.

I didn't know if I would ever be able to swear to her with so little of my queen remaining. Even if that was the only way we could break the curse once and for all.

"I unlocked what had been shut for over a thousand years.

Even more importantly, I forced Arthur from a blood circle he'd infiltrated. We wounded him. We hurt him." She gripped the crescent moon dangling from her throat, and I smelled her blood welling up. "I may not be as strong as her, but I have powerful allies she never had. I have friends ready and willing to do anything to help us."

Despite my reservations, my mouth watered. Her blood bloomed like the rarest moonflower that only graced Tír na nÓg's sparkling shores.

She smelled the same. She smelled like Guinevere. If her blood tasted the same...

I didn't have fangs. I was no vampire Blood.

I didn't have a sword. I'd never been a knight of the Round Table.

I was Merlinus Caledonesis, called a wizard by mankind who feared my power. Legends said I was born demonic, my father an incubus who raped my human mother.

They were right.

Though my father had been dark fae, not the horned boogeyman the priests feared.

"There's no use crying about all that we lost, including Guinevere. Because you're alive, Merlin. I'm alive. Lancelot, Bors, and Mordred survived against all odds to reach me. We have a chance to end this once and for all, but I need you with me." Her eyes flared, her words ringing with conviction.

I saw the beginning of her power revealing itself in the pearly nimbus spreading around her. The cold opal of starlight. The crazed power of the full moon. The bite of frozen snow. But the White Enchantress' greatest power had always been the might of her love. She'd shone like a beacon from the top of Glastonbury Tor, illuminating the marshy moors for miles.

"I will bleed for you." Low and intent, her voice vibrated with each word. "I will fight for you. I will love you with every fiber of my being. Because she saw this moment. She sent you here to wait for *me*. Whether you like it or not, I'm the future that Guinevere died for. She died to ensure I would stand here now, fighting to keep us all alive."

A cloud of white butterflies swept past me to flutter around her head, forming a living crown.

Reluctantly, I stepped closer. Unable to resist the siren call of her blood. Desperate to feel even one moment of her love again.

She held her wounded hand out to me, dripping blood onto the ground that instantly turned into sparkling rubies. I didn't need to glance at her alpha to know he was glaring at me, silently insisting I go to my knees before her.

But only Guinevere had ever held such respect in my heart.

"It's alright," Gwen whispered, whether to me or to her Blood, I wasn't sure.

Darkness rose inside me, casting a shadow across her face. The butterflies huddled together, terrified in the presence of even a half-blood dark fae. I was an abomination in many ways, especially here. A thousand and more years of captivity in paradise had done little to tame the darkness in me.

It had only made me hunger for more. Pain. Terror. Blood.

At heart, I was a creature of nightmare. Not pretty flowers and butterflies. The perfect mask of civility that I'd honed over the centuries slipped, promising unending suffering.

I expected her to flinch and pull away. To duck behind Lancelot. To seek his protection and assurance.

Instead, Gwen smiled, her eyes hardening with a wicked glee that shocked what little of Merlin the man remained.

"Oh yes," she whispered, smiling. "That's exactly what I need to destroy Arthur once and for all."

All my hesitation melted away as the dark creature crawled out of me. My heritage. My shame. The demonic half of me that only Guinevere had ever seen and accepted.

Until Gwen. She pressed her palm to my mouth, lined with jagged shards of obsidian and allowed me to feast.

14

MORDRED

My queen and Lance stepped through the shimmering curtain together, with Bors just a step behind them. One moment, I felt Bors' fierce determination driving him forward, his lungs burning as if already starved for oxygen. He fully expected to drown again as they passed through, yet he still went.

He'd go anywhere our queen led. He would face any fear. So would I.

The next moment, they were gone. The curtain dissolved to nothing. My bond thinned so suddenly that I couldn't do anything but mentally scramble in desperation. I clung to Bors' shoulder as long as I could, but he simply dissolved into thin air.

Gone. My queen was gone. I couldn't feel her in my head at all.

The lake did not know *my* name and refused to allow me to pass. My worst fear. My nightmare.

The legends differed about my role in King Arthur's tale, but one thing remained the same. When it came time to battle him at Camlann, I was alone.

Lancelot and Bors had galloped toward the burning tower. They'd gone to save her, even knowing it was too late. We'd heard her screams in our heads long after she died. Felt her pain searing our flesh. Her agony etched in our bones. Inconsolable grief and rage had driven Lance toward madness, and he'd been unable to return to exact his revenge on Arthur.

He'd left that honor to me. And I'd failed.

Oh, sure, the legends said that I had been the one to deal him the mortal blow, and I'd certainly tried to rip his black heart out of his chest with my talons, but I couldn't pierce dragon hide.

When my queen died, I was nothing. I had no power. My golden eagle was caged. I lost all hope. My love died. My brethren were lost, and the hope of the Round Table and shining Camelot were destroyed.

I'd crumpled to my knees with Guinevere's last wail. I'd sobbed with her. I'd begged our Lady to spare her. To take me instead.

I didn't want to be left behind. I didn't want to live without her. Alone. Lost.

Arthur had stood over me and laughed. He laughed as our queen burned. As she screamed in our heads. Begging us to save her, and failing that, to avenge her.

With what? Our bare hands?

"Ah, Mordred," a familiar voice echoed down the passageway toward me. A voice that blasted my innards with blistering hatred. "So we meet again, at last, at last. Are you going to come out and face your rightful king, sir knight? Or will you cower on your knees again, crying for your lost queen?"

My bond was gone. I couldn't feel even a hint of Gwen or her Blood. But I had to warn them. Somehow.

My mighty eagle screamed with fury, but I didn't shift.

Not yet, at least. I'd have to choose the moment I called forth my talons and beak carefully, because if he was already a dragon, I'd only be a tasty morsel.

Gwen would be lucky to find a single remnant of a tail feather on the ground.

In this day and age, I wasn't a knight. I had no armor. No sword. But I would never go into any dangerous situation without being prepared. I pulled out my satellite phone and texted Gwen's assistant, Kevin Bloom, who'd been left in charge at the tower.

We have a situation. Gwen, L and B passed to Avalon. I'm at Newgrange and Arthur's here. Alert the Isador queen and see if she can reach Gwen to warn her.

Kevin texted back. *Shara will try to get a warning to her. Hold on a sec.*

"Don't make me tear this ancient monument apart to get to you, Mordred," Arthur growled. He slammed against the outer wall, and some of the stones fell out of place. The whole structure rattled, thousands of pounds of stone and earth above my head.

"I'm coming. I'm unarmed. I'm alone."

"I know." I heard the sneer in his voice. "It's only ever you and me in the end. But I assure you that this Camlann ends your miserable existence once and for all."

I slowly walked back toward the entrance, waiting for Kevin's text. "We heard you were busy in Turkey. How'd you convince the Mother of All Dragons to let you go?"

As I neared the entrance, I slowed my pace even more, watching Arthur pace back and forth. Agitated, he stomped and whirled the other direction. He raked a hand through his hair. He wore no clothes, which made sense if he'd flown here as the dragon. But how had he sensed where we were going? He didn't have a bond with Gwen, and we'd neutralized Elaine.

For all his cocky words, his manner was off. He moved…
gingerly. Almost as if he hurt deep inside.

I fought down the tender hope that sprouted. I had to
assume that he was just as vicious and powerful as always.
He was the once and future king for a reason.

No one had been able to fully defeat him and end his
curse upon my queen in over a thousand years.

Though I could only gleefully hope that Tiamat had used
him so hard and well that his dragon was a bit bruised and
weakened.

Kevin's text popped up. *Shara says the bond is very thin, but
she believes she was able to warn Gwen. The Morrígan sends Her
regards.*

I wasn't sure what that meant, but any help from the
Phantom Queen would be welcome. We were in Ireland, and
some accounts had Her married to the Dagda, so it made
sense that She might wish to intervene, even if Gwen didn't
descend from Her house.

A gust of wind blew past me. From *inside* the mound,
behind me. The wind screeched so viciously that I clamped
my hands over my ears. Wings fluttered around me, beating
furiously, brushing past me in a flurry. The stream went on
and on. Thousands of birds, a swirling black horde of crows
that swarmed the man outside.

They pecked at his head and face, making him fling up his
arms to shield his eyes. Talons raked his abdomen and chest.
He howled with rage and the dragon exploded up out of him.

The red beast was massive. He grew and grew, his tail
wrapping around the side of the mound. For all I knew, he
was big enough to enclose the entire site in his bulk. The
crows withdrew but lined up into a perfect black line that
disappeared around the mound.

A circle of crows, perfectly drawn by the goddess Herself
in charcoal.

Hissing out a plume of noxious smoke, the dragon chuckled. "Do you actually think this will stop me from cracking you open and feasting on your heart? I gained new power from Tiamat. I don't need to cross these filthy beasts to go anywhere."

I texted Kevin. *I'm going to try and get him to take me away from here so Gwen can exit safely.*

Then I opened a new message for my queen. *I love you. Always. Be free.*

On a whim, I called Kevin and left the line open as I laid the phone down on the ground and stepped outside. Maybe he would overhear something that would help Gwen stay alive. "I'm here. Do what you wish with me but leave my queen alone. Let her end this with Elaine once and for all."

"This will never be finished." The dragon's words were garbled with hisses, but I could understand him. "Not until she's mine."

"She'll never—"

He lunged forward, knocking me down with one giant wing so he could pin me by my throat beneath foot-long talons. "She. Is. Mine!"

"Not this time!" I panted with pain, trying not to shred myself open even more. Blood spilled from my mouth with each breath. I knew very well how to anger the beast. The one thing Arthur couldn't abide. "Lancelot du Lac will keep her safe!"

Belching dragon fire into the night, he tightened his talons, nearly beheading me. But he took the bait. "If she wants you back alive, then she can come to Glastonbury Tor. One Blood's life for another. I think that's fair, don't you?"

I refused to answer, even if I could have managed to choke out a word through the blood. She would never give Lance to Elaine. Not for me. Not for Bors. Not for anyone.

If she stayed alive and free, then nothing else mattered.

The dragon lowered his head, peering into my face with suspicion. "You die, Mordred. Yet you smile. Don't you realize that I've won? It's impossible for her to escape me this time. Since I fertilized the Mother Dragon's eggs for Her, I can travel through space and time in the blink of an eye. I can see Guinevere wherever she is on this earth. As soon as she returns, I'll know. I'll return. As foretold by Merlin himself, I am the Once and Future King. Even he can't stop me from making Guinevere my queen once more!"

"Pompous. Windbag." I gasped weakly, trying to draw him down closer. "Sir Thomas Malory made that shit up."

"Lies," the dragon snarled.

Closing my eyes, I shifted to my golden eagle as quickly as possible. I focused all my strength. All my love. Even though I knew how this would end. I knew it was impossible. I still had to try.

I whipped my talons up to the dragon's chest and dug in. Hard. Shredding. Tearing. I would find his shriveled heart and rip it out. If he had one.

I must have passed out. The world blurred. Darkness filled my vision but returned in waves. A heavy weight pressed against my chest, making it impossible for me to breathe.

A woman squatted beside me. Shaking her head, she tsked. "You've made so much work for me, Mordred. You're almost beyond my ability to heal. And what have you done to our king?"

Elaine Shalott had always possessed the kind of beauty that inspired men to dedicate poems to her, but she had the look of someone too sickly to ever go outdoors. Her skin was ghostly pale, stark against her raven-black hair pulled into a fierce bun. Black clothes washed her skin out even more, giving her a ghastly appearance. Even in the twenty-first century, she wore her grief like a Victorian widow.

Mourning the loss of a man who would never love her.

I laughed, spluttering on my own blood. "Still half sick of shadows, I see."

She lifted her right hand, each finger flashing in the moonlight like knives. Then she shoved those blades through my torn throat, and I knew no more.

15

GWEN

My great wizard was a demon, or rather, dark fae. Guinevere had been the one to imprison him all this time. She was part fae. So that meant *I* was part fae, though certainly diluted after so many generations. I wasn't even sure what that meant yet or what that changed, if anything at all.

I wasn't sure how long Merlin fed, but my knees trembled. Lance slipped his arm around my waist, supporting me. Bors stepped closer, offering his throat. And yes, I wanted to taste him and Lance again, but they weren't the ones I needed to feed on now.

Merlin lifted his head. A thick tar-like substance oozed and dripped from his angular body. Even the smallest of movements was sharp and jerky, as if his joints were in the wrong places. Or he was made of glass that wouldn't bend. His eyes glittered like obsidian saucers and his mouth was a mess of glass-like teeth. He didn't bite me, but I could only imagine how sharp those teeth were. How much it would hurt.

"Forgive me, my queen." He didn't have human expressions any longer, and his voice carried a sharpness that cut through my head, making me wince. "I can't shift back yet. This form hasn't revealed itself since I stepped through the veil, and it hungers."

With my blood burning in his stomach, I could sense his emotions. Shame tasted foul and rotten on his tongue. He took great pride in his elegant appearance as Merlin, so revealing this demonic side embarrassed him. Worse, I needed to feed so I could solidify our new bond, but he hated exposing me to his dark form. Even Guinevere had struggled to embrace him like this.

That alone steeled my determination. I needed Merlin's bond. I needed him whole and powerful in my Blood. And yeah, maybe I wanted to prove myself just as capable—if not more so—than his beloved queen whom I resembled so very little.

I closed my fingers around his nape, slipping a little in the black oil that coated his skin. Before I could think about it too much, I leaned down and sank my fangs into his throat. For a moment, I was afraid my fangs would just glance off his body. He might look sharp and hard, but his flesh gave way just like Lance's or Bors'.

However, his blood didn't taste like blood at all. Searingly hot, his blood was thick like honey and slightly bitter. Dark chocolate without any sugar. Tea or coffee that had brewed too long and almost burned dry. A bit charred, like ash.

But there was also a wildness that intoxicated me. Sultry heat and darkest temptation. Black velvet and satin, sweat and pain and blood.

Forbidden pleasure. The kind of pain that was oh-so good, almost too much, dancing along that line of agony and bliss.

:*Gwen,*: Shara's voice whispered inside me so faintly that I almost couldn't hear her at all. :*Mordred's in trouble.*:

I jerked my head up, shaking off the lingering sensation of velvet crawling through my veins. I tried to find Mordred's bond, but it was so faint. So thin. I'd assumed that was because of the veil, but what if he was hurt? Badly? "We need to get back. Now. Mordred's in danger."

Which meant that Arthur had returned, despite our belief he'd be with Tiamat long enough for me to slip past Elaine to free Merlin.

Merlin caught my hand and slipped a thin ring onto the ring finger on my right hand. "The weapon that will defeat Arthur, my queen. Forged in fae magic, the same as Excalibur."

The ring looked impossibly old, the design faded as if someone had worn it for hundreds of years. I could barely make out two clasped hands.

"It's a fede ring, a symbol of eternal friendship or love. If you can get close to Arthur, touch this ring to his."

"That's it?" Bors said doubtfully. "You don't want us to cut off his entire hand or something?"

Merlin gnashed his teeth in a ghastly sound that sent chills down my spine. "You're welcome to try, Sir Bors, but methinks it'll be difficult to cut off anything when you're half a dozen pieces in his gullet. The only one we know for sure he won't eat at first glance is our queen."

"That's far from reassuring," Lance grumbled. "Goddess only knows what he'll do to her before she can touch the rings."

Panic trembled the foundations of my mind. If Mordred was dead... If my Blood were already being picked off one by one...

No. I stiffened my spine and pushed my fear and doubt away. Shara had managed to warn me, so I could return in time to save him. Arthur wouldn't want him dead right away. He'd use him somehow.

Bait.

And the only place he'd want me to go…

I turned to Lance and cupped his cheek. "Can I convince you to stay here until this is finished?"

His eyes flared with shock that I would even think to ask such a thing. "You know I cannot. I will not. Use me, my queen. If the opportunity arises, let me be a decoy so you can get closer to Arthur. Once he's dealt with, I know you can undo whatever *she* has done."

Could I, though? You couldn't undo mental and emotional trauma. I might be able to heal his body, but his mind was already damaged from abuse she'd dealt him in previous lifetimes.

"I can handle the Lady of Shadows," Merlin said with a particularly nasty grin.

"Right," Bors drawled, deliberately shuddering. "So we exit from the Chalice Well. Arthur will be waiting with her. Mordred's probably injured pretty badly, though he managed to get word to the Isador queen. Merlin's going to entertain *her*. What do you want Lance and I to do in order to get you close enough to Arthur?"

"We annoy the fuck out of him," Lance said. "He can't abide the mere sight of me."

My mind raced a moment. Something tickled the back of my mind. A memory. Or maybe something Lance had said to me once. I watched as one of the white butterflies hovered in front of me, trying to still my mind so I could think.

Its wings were as large as my palm and paper thin. I thought it was mostly white, but as I looked closer, I noticed spots of red scattered among the delicate wings and fuzz of its body. Like drops of blood splattered on snow. The butterfly flickered, going almost completely transparent, wings drooping and fluttering weakly.

As if it needed to feed.

I lifted my hand, letting it rest on my palm. Bending my thumb closer to it, I silently offered it the same wound I'd offered Merlin. I didn't bleed much now, but there was still a drop of blood welling on the pad of my thumb.

Its little legs gripped my thumb, surprisingly firm and scratchy. It jerked closer and I yelped and jumped.

The little fucker bit me. Hard. As if it had tarantula fangs.

Morgan smiled apologetically. "They've missed you, sister."

The butterfly's wings fluttered harder as the creature fed on me. I could feel it sucking, pulling my blood from the small puncture. I still couldn't believe such a small thing hurt so badly, but I endured it.

Lines of red began to flow across the delicate white wings, connecting the seemingly random droplets that had looked like blood.

When the pattern came together, I gasped. "A dragon."

Morgan lifted her eyebrows, a quizzical smile on her lips. "You didn't know? They were once your, I mean Guinevere's, favorite creature on the isle."

The fanged butterfly abruptly darted away. I raised my thumb, not surprised to see it was red and throbbing. Maybe it had injected me with some kind of anticoagulant or something.

Lance lifted my sore thumb to his mouth and lightly kissed it and then the back of my knuckles. "And you, my queen. How will you approach Arthur to get close to him?"

I sighed. "I'm going to give him exactly what he wants."

16

GWEN

I couldn't see Bors' body, but his fingers stretched up through the water splashing around the fountain. Thankfully, his bond was calm. He'd jumped through the water quickly and hadn't drowned or experienced any lingering discomfort passing through the veil.

I took his hand and allowed him to pull me below the surface. The water was warm and thick, sparkling with energy against my skin. In a matter of seconds, my head broke the surface and the world spun crazily a moment as my senses flipped upside down and around.

He grabbed me beneath my arms and hauled me up out of the water, lightly setting me beside the nested circular pools of the Chalice Well.

As soon as my feet touched the ground, a brilliant flash seared my eyeballs and a gut-wrenching shriek made my eardrums ache. Elaine's alarm.

"Sorry." He grimaced, reaching down through the well to bring Lance through next. "Didn't think about what would trigger it."

"It's alright. They knew we were coming. That's why he brought Mordred here."

Lance dropped down beside me, immediately gathering me closely against him. Bors hovered on my other side. My beloved knights, shielding me with their bodies when they had no armor. Mordred's bond already flickered like a weak candle, almost extinguished.

If they died…

I pushed that overwhelming, soul-sucking dread aside. I couldn't contemplate failure. Not this time.

Guinevere's curse ends. Now.

Merlin's shadow peeled away from the well like a shiny black oil slick. Head falling back, arms spread wide, he breathed deeply, nostrils flaring, mouth gaping open to taste the air itself. "Ahhhh." He licked his lips as he lowered his head. "It's good to be back among the sheep. I will need to feed before I can change back to my less intimidating form."

"I didn't think you fed like us," I said slowly.

His teeth weren't for puncturing and drinking blood. All those jagged saw-like blades were more suited for tearing.

"I don't." He shrugged. "I'm dark fae."

I didn't really care what he needed to do to sustain himself, but I was thankful he didn't provide any gruesome details. "Hopefully before the sun rises, I'll provide you with a feast."

His large, circular eyes gleamed in the moonlight. "Guinevere forbade me the pleasure of dining on her king, or I would have eliminated him long before he gained so much power."

"When I'm finished with him, you have my full permission to dine on any part of him that interests you."

He inclined his head reverently. "My queen, I live to serve."

I started to incline my head too, but a weight shifted on

top of my head, surprising me. Maybe one of the butterflies was tangled in my hair. Wary of their teeth, I reached up gingerly, but my fingers settled on something cold and hard.

I leaned over the well, trying to see my reflection. A three-pronged crown sat on my head with large wing-like pieces that swept back over my ears. It was hard to tell for sure, but it looked like it was made from dark, shiny crystal rather than metal.

Maybe even the same material of Merlin's dark fae form.

"The butterflies turned into a crown when you passed through the veil." Lance tucked my hand beneath his arm, gently turning me to face our enemies. He raised his voice to a rolling boom that echoed across the land. "The Once and Future Queen of Camelot has returned!"

We'd agreed that Lance would do everything in his power to stir Arthur's anger. I just hadn't expected him to start out quite so directly.

The dragon belched flames across the sky, singing two ancient yew trees that stood as sentinels on either side of the cobbled path to the well. He raked the ground with both front feet, tearing massive grooves and ruts into the beautiful garden. His tail crashed through an ivy-covered bower with a swing tucked inside.

A woman stood off to our right, well away from his wings and swiping tail. Elaine's pale face flickered through the darkness like a ghost. It was no surprise to any of us that she stared at Lancelot, wholly focused on him.

His fingers tightened on mine, but he didn't otherwise react at her nearness.

A dark shape lay on the ground at her feet. :Mordred? I'm here. Hang on.:

He didn't answer, but I could still feel his bond, so I wasn't too late. I didn't dare draw my blood yet so I could heal him, but hopefully he could hold on a bit longer.

I waited a moment for Arthur's dragon to cease bellowing so he could hear me. "It always surprises me to see a grown man throw such a temper tantrum."

"You always did have a pretty mouth," he growled out, still fuming arid smoke. "Too bad you never learned to shut it."

An ugly memory flickered up through the generations that Guinevere had endured this curse. Squeezing her throat, he glared down at her, forcing her to her knees. *"Show your king how sorry you are for disrespecting me before our knights. Open that pretty mouth and put it to better use."*

Shuddering, I pushed that image away. He wanted to remind me of our past. To put me in my place. Drunk on power from the dark ring, he was so used to controlling and shaming Guinevere that he had nothing to fear.

He didn't fear retaliation from me, even with four of my Blood bonds strengthening my power. Even with Shara and her sibling bonds at my disposal. He hadn't learned a thing from our demonstration when we'd forced him out of the Isador blood circle.

That was how arrogant he was. How stupid. How blindly confident that the ring on his finger would be enough to suppress anything I managed to throw at him.

So... I played along. I needed to get close, and I wouldn't give him a reason to suspect a thing. Until it was too late.

"I've been told that I'm merely a shadow of the queen that Guinevere used to be. I don't have anywhere near her power."

I couldn't see Merlin any longer—he'd disappeared into the shadows beneath the trees. But I felt the cut of my words in his bond like jagged shards of broken glass. *:Forgive me, my queen.:*

:You're right, so there's nothing to forgive.:

The dragon let out a chuckling hiss. "That sounds like

something Merlin would say. I see she finally let you out of Avalon. How'd the demon enjoy the land of paradise?"

"Very well indeed." Merlin's voice crackled like shattered glass beneath heavy boots. His voice was already well ahead of us, close enough to Elaine that she shrank back against one of the mighty trees, though she couldn't tear her gaze from Lance.

Interesting. I didn't know why she was afraid of Merlin.

:We have a very long history, my queen. She's as dark as I am, though her glamor fades. It'll be a pleasure to finally reveal her true form.:

"You made an offer to me in the Isador Tower," I said calmly. "I would like to discuss your compromise further. That's why I come here willingly. None of us have attacked you or tried to defend ourselves. I want to parley."

Lance stiffened and jerked his head around to glare at me, but he didn't say a word.

I definitely had the dragon's interest too. He gave me a sly look that made chills slither down my spine. "I'm listening."

"You wanted us to be Arthur and Guinevere again. I'd hoped that by calling my Blood that I'd regain some of her former glory, but I'm barely a shell of the queen she used to be. I don't want to lose my Blood again. I don't want to watch you kill them. I don't want to die in misery and be reborn even weaker."

The dragon sat up on his haunches and gave me a bored, heavy-lidded look as if he'd suddenly gotten very sleepy. He lifted his massive paw and licked his foot-long claws one by one. "What do you propose?"

I swallowed hard, letting my reluctance show on my face. My dread would only excite him. My fear would arouse him.

He wanted me to come crying and begging to plead for my Bloods' lives.

So I had better make this a damned good show.

"I'll give you what you want. I'll help you bring Camelot back."

He yawned, gaping his mouth wide so that I would flinch back in fear. "What is it that I want, Guinevere? I want to hear you say it."

"I will marry you, Arthur. I will be your queen and wife again. I ask only that you spare my Blood."

"Hmmmm," he drawled out a rumbling sigh. "I'm afraid it's probably too late for poor Mordred. I believe he's beyond even Guinevere's healing, my dear, and if you're a shell of her, then he's surely dead."

I closed my eyes and let my emotions wash over me. Tears. Trembling lips. Shuddering breath. I didn't hide how much the thought of losing him hurt me, though I held his bond tighter in my mind. *:Don't listen to him, Mordred. I can and will heal you. I promise.:*

"Lance," I ground out. "Bors. Merlin. Spare them, at least."

Arthur turned slitted dragon eyes on Lance. "Alphas and kings rarely get along."

:Especially when said king is a psychotic asshole,: Bors growled in our bonds.

"Besides, I have to fulfill my promise to the Lady of Shalott."

He didn't give a crap about keeping his promises. We all knew it. He'd lied and cheated and conned his way through Camelot even before the shining walls fell.

Lance didn't say a word, but a quiver rocked his entire frame before he managed to conceal it. "If it means my queen lives and the rest of her Blood are allowed to guard her, then you can do whatever you wish with me."

A rumbling purr rolled from the dragon's chest. "Prove it."

Lance gathered up my hand and raised my knuckles to his mouth. "My queen."

Then my shining knight released me and strode toward his greatest nightmare. He didn't hesitate. He didn't glance back over his shoulder at me.

He dropped down on one knee before Elaine and bowed his head. "My lady, how may I serve?"

Outwardly, he looked completely calm and reserved. But his bond iced over in my head. Blizzard winds blew blinding snow through his mind. So cold. Frozen. Dead.

Lancelot du Lac would always defend me. His honor demanded nothing less than perfect chivalry and love.

Even if it meant surrendering to our enemy to make sure that I lived.

"Lancelot," she whispered reverently. "Is it really you?"

"It is I, my lady." To most people, his demeanor would have looked normal. But I heard the slight catch in each word. The shallow, too rapid breaths. She held her hand out to him and he took it, though he couldn't hide the slight tremble in his fingers. He even kissed the back of her hand, though he kept his head low.

Hiding the frozen dread and horror in his eyes. Though knowing her, she would probably relish that look of fear in his eyes as much as Arthur wanted mine.

"It's your turn, my dear," the dragon drawled in a voice that oozed with slimy satisfaction.

Head high, I slowly walked toward him. Tears dripped down my cheeks, but I went as calmly and proudly as Lance had gone to *her*. I curtsied, albeit stiffly, and managed to ground out, "My lord."

He lowered his massive head and deliberately blew smoke in my face. Choking, I turned my head away, but I didn't take a step back or flinch. One big paw settled over my shoulder, claws digging into my flesh.

He didn't care that I bled.

An Aima queen, descended from the goddess, ripe with the power of my Blood.

He. Didn't. Care.

Fool.

I didn't act. Yet. For all I knew, it was a deliberate ploy to get me to betray myself, so he'd have a reason to kill my Blood one by one while making me watch.

One talon snagged the bodice of my gown, giving it a teasing tug. Cheeks burning, I pushed his giant paw away. "At least shift back before you touch me."

He jerked up on his hind legs, making my heart thunder desperately. Power flowed through me, a shining river begging to be used. I almost reached for it. I almost defended myself.

Especially when Lance cried out softly.

My alpha. Fucking *whimpered.*

I bit my lip, uncaring that blood dripped down my chin. I fought the urge to race to him. To turn and see what Elaine had done to make such a vulnerable, terrified sound escape my proud alpha's lips.

The dragon shrank, folding up on itself until only Arthur remained before me. He still smelled like a rutting feral dragon. The odor made me wrinkle my nose, and I averted my face when he leaned down to kiss me. I couldn't help it. "You positively reek of dragon sex."

He had the grace to withdraw. In fact, he actually blushed slightly and raked a hand through his hair. "Tiamat used the dragon hard, I'm afraid. I'll bathe in the Chalice Well after we consummate our union."

Such a sacrilege. The Chalice Well had always been associated with the Mother. I didn't imagine that She'd be pleased to have such a man sullying Her sacred waters.

"You still haven't proven your willingness to be my bride, Guinevere."

I clenched my jaws. Lips tight, I looked up into his face.

He leered at me and planted his hands on his hips. I didn't have to drop my gaze to his groin to know that he was aroused. It was no surprise to any of us that he'd be excited at the prospect of humiliating me in front of my Blood. Of using me. Hurting me.

Nothing got him off like abusing Guinevere, especially if he could do it in front of people who actually cared about her wellbeing.

Swallowing hard, I dropped to my knees in front of him.

"No," Bors growled. "Don't."

Arthur snarled at him. "Take a step closer, Sir Bors. Just one step. Let me show you how quickly your head can be parted from your body."

I closed my eyes. I allowed my shoulders to shake. My breathing sounded loud in the silence, desperate gulps just shy of sobs. Without opening my eyes, I grabbed at his hips and leaned in slightly. Shifting my hand up his thigh. Higher. The tips of his fingers.

Yes.

I closed my right hand over his and threaded our fingers together in a semblance—a mockery—of our union.

Which put my fede ring against the ring he'd stolen from Tylwyth Teg.

My ears rang and throbbed, but I didn't physically hear anything. My hair lifted from my nape and electricity rippled up my arm, stinging needles as if my hand had touched a live socket.

"What the fuck?" His arm jerked, but I squeezed tighter, keeping the rings pressed together.

Frantic, he punched me repeatedly with his other hand until he managed to knock me back sprawling on my ass. Glaring at me with murderous fury, he roared, "What have you done?"

17

LANCE

In my head, I crawled away into the darkest corner I could find. It shamed me to my core, but I couldn't face the monster that stood over me. She cupped my cheek and she might as well have sliced my chest, cracked open my ribs, and fingered my heart. I shuddered. I gasped. Cold sweat slicked my hair to my forehead.

I knew it was ridiculous to have such a bad reaction to a simple, seemingly innocent touch. But my body remembered not so innocent touches from this woman. I remembered being drugged. I remembered being bound by magic to a bed and not allowed to leave for months. A year. Maybe longer.

My mind flinched away, unable to examine the dark holes where those memories lurked.

"Elaine." Merlin's voice echoed from all directions. "The Lady of Shalott. Have you looked in a mirror lately?"

"No," she whispered hoarsely, her fingers digging into my cheek. She pressed closer to me, her other arm frantically clutching at my shoulders. "Protect me, Lancelot. Don't let him hurt me."

"Where is your magic web, Elaine? Have you figured out what your curse is yet?"

She smelled of rose water and lemon verbena. Scents that threw me back to a dark tower room. My hands and feet bound to the bed frame. Her hair flowing over my face, drying my tears.

I gagged, averting my face. But I didn't push her away from me.

"No mirrors," she babbled frantically, ducking her face against my shoulder. "I forbade them. I won't even look at my image in the well. You can't make me."

A cold hand settled on my back, though she couldn't see Merlin behind me. It was dark here beneath the giant yew, and his form blended perfectly with the shadows. :Say 'Tirra Lirra.':

I had no idea what that meant but I immediately said the words out loud. "Tirra Lirra."

Her head jerked up, her eyes flaring wide. Her mouth fell open with shock.

Leaning over my shoulder, Merlin stared into her eyes. "Look into my mirrors, Elaine Shalott. See your shadows once more."

She wailed, a wretched sound that made even me pity her. Shaking against me, she seemed to wither. Her hair tumbled free, creeping from black to stony gray and then yellowed white. Her pale face tightened, her eyes sunken hollows. Her lips blackened, her teeth jagged and sharp like Merlin's. Though she didn't have the same shiny black form that looked like shards of obsidian.

"Depart the earthly plane," Merlin ordered. "Return to your tower, foul creature."

She fell backwards, her arms and legs cracking and bending at odd angles. Scuttling like a crab, she staggered away. No, not a crab. A spider.

Tumbling over the edge of the pool, she disappeared into the Chalice Well with a splash.

Merlin helped me to my feet. Thankfully, he didn't say anything remotely sympathetic, or I might have blubbered like a child. "Don't be a bloody idiot and say those words ever again. They'll call her straight to you once more."

I shuddered, even though I had no idea what the words meant. "Got it."

My legs still felt like jelly, but I made myself start moving toward Gwen. Goddess above, she was on her knees. A naked Arthur stood over her.

An ugly, murderous rage pulsed through me. Bors didn't have to tell me what the king had demanded from her.

Head back, Arthur quivered as if a lightning bolt had blasted him. Not in ecstasy, thank goddess. The only part Gwen touched was his hand.

She'd done it.

"Did it work?" I asked hoarsely.

Merlin hmphed. "You doubt *me*, the great and powerful wizard of Camelot? Of course it fucking worked. I'm no apprentice, believe it or not."

Tearing his hand free, Arthur staggered backwards. He jerked and twitched helplessly in the throes of whatever magic Merlin had worked. Soft balls of light popped up from the ring. With each one, he shuddered and gasped, quivering as if each one pained him.

"Souls," Merlin said grimly. "The dead he's gathered over the centuries, plus the ones that Gwyn had gathered before Arthur stole the ring. They're free now."

The balls danced and hovered above our heads. Some of them shot toward the Chalice Well, but others floated up toward Glastonbury Tor. The top of the ancient tower flashed and shone like a lighthouse, beaming with the souls of the dead.

Arthur's shoulders drooped, but the ring wasn't finished with him yet. It slipped off his finger and clattered on the stone paving. White light poured from the ring, bright enough that I had to squint and shield my eyes. Slowly, the glowing light took on an identifiable form.

White flowing wings, as large as the red dragon's. Glossy and delicate transparent butterfly wings of liquid moonlight. Long sinuous neck. Splatters of red gleamed like rubies on the wings.

"Guinevere," Gwen breathed reverently. "The White Enchantress."

The wings stretched out to their full breadth, fluttering through the giant yews and across the gardens without causing any damage. The deep furrows that Arthur had torn into the earth smoothed. The charred leaves sprouted with new growth. And Mordred climbed to his feet, rubbing his neck.

"Red and white dragons fought tonight." Sweet and high, Guinevere's voice brought tears to my eyes. I knew that voice. Even though I'd never heard it before. My soul recognized her, as if even now, I carried a few drops of our ancient queen's blood. "This time, white has reigned victorious. Thank you, Gwenhwyfar Findabair. The curse is complete."

I took the last few steps to reach my queen, and together, we four Blood dropped to our knees around her.

Gwen. Our living queen. Free at last.

Gossamer wings fluttered over us like kisses from an angel. "Merlinus, make sure the ring is returned to Tylweth Teg."

He pressed his face to the ground. "At once, Your Majesty."

The shining white dragon with fluttering butterfly wings hovered closer to our queen and bowed her head to lay her cheek against Gwen's. "You are no shell, Gwenhwyfar. I am honored to call you daughter of my daughters. You accomplished what countless queens who came before you could not."

Wings outspread, the dragon soared up into the air, glowing brighter and brighter. So fierce and intense that I had to turn my head. So much power. No wonder Arthur had been so incredibly strong. He'd had Guinevere trapped in the ring all these centuries, using her power to sustain himself.

I fully expected the dragon to go soaring off toward the tower, but a white cannonball shot down from the sky, straight toward Gwen. Wings tucked tight, the dragon slammed into my queen, knocking her off her feet.

We caught her, all four of us. She would never fall as long as we lived. For a moment, the butterfly wings gleamed around her, and then the dragon sank deeper into her body.

"Wow," she breathed, eyes shining with the glow of Guinevere's dragon.

We pressed closer to her. Holding her. Drinking in her scent. Her touch. Her love.

Arthur dropped to his hands and knees, crawling frantically across the cobblestones until he found the ring. He slipped it on his hand and let out a ragged cry. "No. It's gone. The power is gone!"

Without her request, I helped Gwen regain her footing, though none of us rose from our knees. "The power isn't gone, Arthur. It's just not yours any longer."

Before our eyes, the once and future king shrank. No longer tall and strong and young. His dark hair thinned and grayed. His arrogant, handsome face sagged into the heavy jowls of a man who'd indulged for decades. Wine, drugs, women, violence. All the vices were written in his reddened complexion and puffy skin.

"I demand that you return what you've stolen from me,"

he retorted. "We had a deal. I spared your Blood! You can't do this to me!"

Her eyebrows rose slightly. "Oh? I can't? I don't recall any deal. Do you, Lance?"

"Actually, my queen, I do recall something…"

Arthur smoothed his greasy, sparse hair back from his face and lowered his chin belligerently. "See? I told you. Even *he* remembers. You *owe* me, Guinevere."

"You're right. I do owe you. I owe you vengeance." Turning to me, she cupped my cheek. "Would you do me the great honor of acting as my champion, Sir Lancelot?"

I closed my fingers around hers and lifted her hand to my mouth, pressing a kiss against her palm. "It would be my greatest honor, my queen."

Arthur sputtered. "You can't possibly be serious. A challenge? I don't have a champion! This is ridiculous! I don't even have a sword!"

She tipped her head toward the Chalice Well. In a few moments, a glowing sword floated past us to hover before Arthur.

I hadn't seen the weapon with my own eyes before, but there could be no doubt that it was the greatest sword ever forged. Excalibur. It screamed its famous name, slowly spinning in midair. Silvery-blue runes glistened up and down its perfect blade. A large white crystal spun rainbows from its pommel.

Even in this day and age, humans remembered the legendary tale of Arthur pulling the sword from the stone.

This sword.

I had the insane urge to kiss the cold steel of its blade and beg its forgiveness for even thinking of challenging its bearer.

Grimacing, Arthur wrapped his hand around the great sword's hilt as skillfully as a toddler picking up a fork for the first time. "Very well. I hate to make you cry on our wedding day, Guinevere."

The idiot still thought he could win. A challenge. Against Lancelot du Lac?

Bors snorted. Merlin licked his lips, eyes shining hungrily.

Mordred looked around at all of us and let out a disgusted grunt. "Fucking hell. Didn't anyone bring popcorn?"

"My name is Gwen," she said firmly, shaking her head. "Oh, the confidence of a mediocre asshole used to getting everything he's ever wanted thanks to someone else's gifts."

I climbed to my feet and unsheathed my sword. "I've waited over a thousand years to do this."

Arthur sneered at me. "To challenge me?"

I smiled and raised the sword over my shoulder, gripping it lightly in both hands. "No. To kill you."

———————

GWEN

I t was far from a fair fight.

No one could face Lancelot du Lac in a duel and win. Not when he held a sword. Even when his opponent wielded the legendary Excalibur.

The original King Arthur had surely fared better with a sword in his hand than this man before me now, or he never would have gained his knights' respect. He charged recklessly, swinging the elegant sword like a club. Lance easily sidestepped each blow, or simply leaned out of the way. He let Arthur swing and hack until he was red-faced and wheezing.

Then Lance smiled and landed the first blow.

I'd seen him beat the shit out of Bors and never draw a single drop of blood. Sir Bors, who was easily one of the best knights of the Round Table second only to Lancelot.

But when Lance swung his sword at Arthur, he made a deep slice across his forearm. Yelping, he clutched the wound and backed away. Only to yelp again when Lance left another cut on his opposite shoulder. His thigh. His side.

Methodically, Lance landed blow after blow, leaving long, bleeding cuts on Arthur's body. None of them were deep. None of them were mortal. Even though he could have easily decapitated his opponent or simply sliced off a limb.

The man who'd honored his best friend by never drawing a single drop of blood, now deliberately set about draining every last drop of blood from his former king with all the skill the goddess had given him.

I almost felt sorry for Arthur. Almost. It took him half a dozen wounds before he realized exactly what Lance was doing to him. Even then, he thought he could bluster his way out.

"I'm your king, Lancelot. I order you to lay down your sword!"

Lance flicked his sword up carelessly, nicking one of Arthur's testicles.

"OW! You fucking moron! How dare you injure your lord and master?"

So Lance left a deeper cut on Arthur's other testicle, nearly separating it from his body.

Staggering in pain, Arthur finally started to look scared. So naturally he turned to me for help.

"Please, call this off, Guinevere. I'll forgive everything. We can still work things out."

Dispassionately, I watched in silence as Lance made a series of quick, sharp cuts that left the letter G carved in Arthur's chest. "My name is Gwen."

He stumbled toward me, hands outstretched to grab me. Maybe to beg for forgiveness—or in a last-ditch effort to use me somehow to sway Lance toward mercy. Before he could lay a single finger on me, Lance dropped a hard, quick blow to stop the attack.

Both of Arthur's severed hands fell to the ground. Before Excalibur could hit the ground, Lance snatched it in his left hand.

Eyes wide with shock, Arthur fell to his knees before me. His mouth opened and closed several times, before he could actually get any words out. "Please. Gwen."

Not even breathing hard, Lance stood behind him and met my gaze. Both swords ready in his hands. With a flick of his wrists, he could easily decapitate Arthur. All he waited for was my order.

:*Do you want the honor of his death?*: I asked him silently.

:*It matters not to me, as long as you're safe, my queen. Do as you will.*:

I stared at the man who'd caused me and my ancestors so much agony. So much grief. I couldn't even begin to understand why he'd tortured us for so long. Why he'd ever thought he was owed a woman's pain. Why he'd even thought to take a queen's power for himself. He'd reveled in our suffering. Even now, he looked at me expectantly, as if any moment I would realize my mistake and beg his forgiveness. He'd fed on pain and darkness all these centuries.

It was time for pain and darkness to feed on him.

"Merlin," I whispered softly.

My dark fae stepped forward. "Aye, my queen?"

"You may now have what I promised you."

"With pleasure, my queen."

Thick shadows enveloped Arthur, writhing eagerly with flashes of sharp obsidian and midnight glass. He shrieked, a high-pitched wail that almost made me cover my ears. But I remembered Guinevere making similar sounds over the generations of the curse as her power faded and Arthur's grew.

His sins had only worsened over the years. No obscenity was forbidden to him. No act of cruelty beneath him.

I made myself stand there and listen while the man who'd tortured my house for generations was devoured by shadow.

The sky brightened, the sun creeping above the horizon before Merlin stood before me a man again. The glittering black form was replaced by the lavender-haired man in perfect elven robes. Though a speck of blood dotted the corner of his mouth.

I rubbed the spot away with my thumb. "Thank you, my Blood."

He bowed low, though he kept his gaze locked to mine. "Thank you, my queen. I've been dreaming of that for almost two thousand years."

Bors slapped him on the shoulder. "Was he at least tasty?"

Merlin grunted. "Fuck, no. He tasted like shit-covered refuse left to rot in the desert a thousand years. May he rot in the pits of Dante's inferno for all eternity."

Laughing, Lance swept me up into his arms. "Amen. Let's go home."

Bors groaned. "Do we have to go through the well again?"

"I am surrounded by incompetent idiots," Merlin growled. "Of course not. We can simply pass through the tower, if you're not too exhausted to climb the tor."

"The ring!" I gasped over Lance's shoulder as he strode out of the garden.

Merlin held up the black signet ring, waving it back and forth. "I've got the foul thing. I can't wait to see it melted into something more useful. Maybe an obsidian urinal in honor of our king. What manner of castle do you command now, my queen?"

"Only a hundred-story tower in the largest and grandest city of America." Lance lifted his hand above his head, and Excalibur floated to him eagerly, like a hound who'd finally found his master. He kissed the hilt and then laid the famous sword on top of me. "As foretold, the Once and Future Queen has truly returned in our time of greatest need."

Bors and Mordred cheered in unison. "Long live the Queen of Camelot!"

Shara Isador needs more queens to come to the table. Meet Karmen in Queen Takes Sunfires Book 1. If you're new to Their Vampire Queen, start with Queen Takes Knights!

ABOUT THE AUTHOR

Shop for book merchandise, sign up for Joely's newsletter, and join the Triune for all of Joely's latest book news, fun giveaways, and upcoming projects!